CW00740434

Emma –
Let's save the world
together.
    Dino – Power!
    J. J.

OSCAR

The dinosaur who saved Earth

To Otter. Thank you for all your love, support and dog walking.

The Discovery

Noah and Luna couldn't believe it! The bright, sharp, beams of light from their climbing helmet lamps sliced through the cave's darkness like lasers. They were lighting up thousands of large, egg-shaped rocks, running in neat rows across the floor of the enormous, freezing-cold cavern that stretched before them.

Bright, sparkling, spring water spilled down from the walls and the stalactites that hung from the cathedral-like cavern they were now standing in. The water kept flowing, just as it had for millions of years, shaping the egg-like rocks with a smooth, solid layer of limestone that melded them all into one. Even so, they were clearly eggs - a lot of gigantic eggs!

Not a sound could be heard in the cave, apart from the relentless, gentle flow of water. Not surprising since they were a long way underground. The eggs had lain here, undisturbed, nearly forever. Finally, the ancient legend of hidden dinosaur eggs in these mountains had been proven true.

Noah's mouth hung open as he kept blinking in disbelief. A few seconds passed before their nervous laughter broke the silence. "Dinosaur eggs!" gasped Luna.

"We are going to need some help to move these," said Noah, his voice rattling eerily around the cave like thunder. "A lot of help..." he trailed off, as the enormity of their discovery started to sink in.

Luna was certain she could see what looked like a light purple luminous glow emanating from some of the eggs. But perhaps this was just a trick of the light? It was very hard to tell in the shadowy half-light of the cave.

"Noah, do you see that? It's like a soft light, a glow or something," whispered Luna.

" Yes, you're right. It's like they have a life of their own," answered Noah, squinting at them.

The two exchanged a series of amazed looks with one another.

"Look, over there. That one has a light purple hue to it," said Luna, pointing.

"Are they...are they glowing? Glittering?" said Noah, simply astonished.

Luna couldn't resist the urge to touch one of the eggs but hesitated.

"Do you think they are safe?" she asked.

"Well if they are dinosaur eggs then they should be completely dormant. But that glow...it's very strange," answered Noah. "They seem to be almost sparkling," he said.

Luna wanted to walk up to the eggs and pick one up. If only she could take it back to their campsite for the scientists that were part of their team to have a closer look at!

"They are mesmerising. I wish we could take one back," said Luna

But the eggs were far too big and heavy to move.

"They're huge. We'd need a team of weightlifters to even budge one," asserted Noah.

As the reality of the situation dawned on them, they broke into more nervous laughter.

Their laughter echoed through the cavern, a mix of disbelief and sheer excitement.

"We better get some rest and grab a bite to eat before we make our way back to tell others," said Luna, trying hard to contain her enthusiasm.

"Yep, I'm really tired," agreed Noah.

A short rest, a piece of carrot cake, and a few gulps of water later, Noah and Luna started off back through the vast complex of caves, pits, caverns, passages, and underground lakes.

Following the same route, they retraced their steps through the narrow passageway. As they journeyed out of the mountain, a sense of déjà vu washed over them, and they found themselves travelling through the hidden world they had discovered only a few hours earlier. By now, both of them were utterly exhausted and feeling really quite cold.

"Race you back," Luna teased Noah with a mischievous look on her face.

"Bet I'll beat you," came Noah's response, as he started sprinting off along the tunnel.

With their hearts racing and the thrill of their amazing discovery still coursing through their veins, Noah and Luna pressed forward. Through the mountain they went, retracing their way back to the camp, manoeuvring over massive rocks and braving icy streams. Luna slipped under the hidden ledge they had discovered a few hours earlier, squeezing through a tight gap to get back into the main cave.

Slowly but steadily, they worked their way towards the team of archaeologists and scientists who were camping on a grass-covered plateau near the cave's entrance. Just the thought of how astonished they will be when they heard what Noah and Luna had discovered, made Luna beside herself with excitement!

Noah looked at Luna, his eyes beaming with admiration. "You're a regular CindyAnna Jones! All you need is a bullwhip and a hat," he quipped.

They kept walking, smiling at each other. What they had done was nothing short of miraculous, and the occasional shared laugh gave away their sense of pride at what they had achieved.

Luna stood out from other kids of her age. She was taller than most girls of 11 years old and as skinny as a skateboard. Her long blonde hair flowed straight down her back when she didn't have it tied up, and she had a wide mouthed smile that could brighten any room. She wore simple, geeky, steel-rimmed glasses, which made her seem a lot more serious than she actually was.

Noah, even taller than Luna, but not quite as skinny, sported the same style of steel-rimmed glasses that Luna wore. His short, wiry, dark hair poked out from under his helmet like spikes. He was almost a year older than Luna and she looked up to him like an older brother.

Both were dressed in professional caving and climbing clothing, complete with sturdy hiking boots to help keep them safe and warm.

Their parents were archaeologists spearheading the expedition with a team of scientists and explorers waiting above ground. Their mission? To unearth hidden dinosaur eggs that had lain dormant for millennia.

Luna and Noah had met each other several summers previously at Harvard University, where Noah's parents both worked as researchers of dinosaurs and other early forms of life. It was there that Luna and Noah had discovered their mutual love of exploring caves and the big outdoors. Since then, they had both been on several adventures together during their holidays. But nothing quite like this!

Luna and Noah had eagerly leapt at the opportunity to be a part of this expedition. For their age, they were both highly experienced at both climbing and caving, so they would be highly useful to the team. And, anyway, who would want to spend the school summer holidays at home indoors on their own, when they could go hunting for dinosaur eggs in the Appalachian Mountains.

And boy, had they had hit the jackpot this time!

CHAPTER 2

Waking the Camp

Some hours later, Luna and Noah finally made it back to the cave's gaping wide entrance where their camp was. The inky, black darkness of the night had enveloped everything, and everyone was sound asleep. The moon bathed the campsite in a silvery glow, creating a strange, otherworldly atmosphere.

Tents of various shapes and sizes dotted the area, spreading across the fields like a patchwork quilt. A spacious field kitchen tent stood at the centre where everyone ate their meals together. The pleasant weather, however, often encouraged many members of the team to enjoy their meals outdoors at one of the many wooden camping tables that littered the grassy plateau the camp sat on.

Under the moon's glow, the tents seemed to contort and bend, creating an eerie scene that made the canvas village seem spooky.

Both Luna and Noah were completely exhausted, their energy drained by the challenging trek into, and back out of, the mountain. But the excitement in their voices betrayed their fatigue.

"I can't wait to tell them!" yelled Luna.

"Let's wake them then," Noah shouted, his laughter echoing as he began striking the kitchen dinner gong repeatedly with gusto. The resounding clang was usually reserved for meals or urgent announcements, but Noah's enthusiasm knew no bounds tonight. Luna's initial surprise quickly turned into a hearty laugh. "You're quite the comedian," she joked, a playful smirk shaping her lips.

Tent after tent flickered into life, as lights illuminated the camp, casting a warm glow in the high mountain darkness. Nestled among the peaks of the mountains, a new story was unfolding! Their remarkable find had started to stir the camp from its slumber, and the news quickly started to ripple through the moonlit campsite.

They understood that their loud and sudden wake-up call might not make them universally popular among everyone in this village of tent-dwellers. But the alternative was waiting till the morning and neither of them had the patience for that.

"You can't make an omelette without cracking a few eggs...dinosaur eggs, that is!" Noah yelled mischievously.

What an amazing day it had been! And it was about to get even more dramatic once everyone had learnt their exciting news.

Luna confidently undid the rope securing the heavy, waxed canvas door to the main tent and stepped into its dark and silent interior and headed straight for the spot where she knew the Professor was sleeping. Professor Brown, the leader of this international expedition team, was highly respected among dinosaur experts worldwide. He was overseeing the entire project at the camp and was in charge of everyone. He was also Luna's father.

Quietly, Luna walked up to the Professor's wooden framed bed and gave his shoulder a gentle shake. He was still dressed in his worn tweed jacket and a comfortable-looking, light blue chequered woollen shirt. "Dad, wake up," Luna whispered urgently. "Dad, Dad!" repeating his name softly to rouse him from his slumber.

A single, heavily wrinkled eye popped open sceptically, much like that of a startled gecko. It peered out from behind a tangle of wild, snowy white hair that stood at an amusingly crooked angle. Luna often referred to her father's hair when it was like this as his 'candy floss hair.'

"What on earth?" the Professor grumbled; his voice tinged with annoyance. He wasn't pleased with being woken from his beauty sleep like this - even by his own daughter.

"We've found them!" Luna blurted out, unable to contain her excitement. "Thousands of them, perfectly preserved! Thousands of dinosaur eggs - three different types from what I could see!"

With a sudden jolt of alertness, the Professor was fully awake. In an instant, he transformed from a suspicious gecko to a wise old owl. With wide eyes and nostrils flared, he enthusiastically flapped his arms like a pair of wings as he sat up in bed.

"Oh my, oh my!" he shrieked.

In a single swift motion, the Professor sprang out of his camping bed, hastily slipping on his walking boots - the only thing he wasn't already wearing in bed. His cheeks turned a vibrant shade of red, his excitement clear to see.

As he smoothed his unruly hair into a vague semblance of order and cleared the sleep from his eyes, his head swivelled, and he suddenly became a whirlwind of activity.

"Oh my! Are you sure? Are you absolutely sure you've found them? Oh my!" he repeated in an abnormally shrill voice. He coughed, trying to correct his voice to a more normal pitch.

"Yes, I'm pretty certain!" confirmed Luna. "There are loads of them Dad, literally thousands of them!"

"Wow! That's amazing Luna. Well done, well done you," he replied, struggling to speak normally.

"Do you want some coffee?" he interrupted. "You must be tired, Luna," the Professor smiled gently at his young daughter. "It's really good coffee," he assured her. He swelled with pride at what Luna had achieved and was glad he had let her 'do her own thing'.

"Yes, please. Thank you, Dad!" Luna replied politely, a grateful smile on her face. To be honest, she wouldn't have been able to tell good coffee from bad coffee. At the moment, anything wet and warm was a welcome comfort. "Two sugars, if you don't mind Dad," she added with a friendly nod.

He began preparing coffee for the two of them, reaching for his favourite blend - freshly ground Blue Mountain from Jamaica. It was a treat he usually saved for remarkable moments, and this certainly qualified as one.

"Feel free to make yourself some toast to go along with it too, darling," the Professor suggested to Luna, his voice warm and encouraging.

Luna toasted some bread and spread butter and thick apricot marmalade on it, a satisfying treat to accompany her coffee. Although her 'survival rations' had kept her going in the cave, the carrot cake had become a tad dry by the time she actually had a chance to sit down and eat it. Hours of exploration deep in the cave had certainly helped her work up her appetite, and she ate the toast quickly, licking her fingers noisily as she did so.

The hot coffee and toast were a delicious combination, and Luna didn't waste a moment savouring every bite. She even used her forefinger to scoop up the last few crumbs from her plate. With a satisfied grin, she proclaimed, "Yummmmmmy!" for all to hear. As she licked her breadcrumbed finger with a loud slurp.

"OK," the Professor declared, his voice carrying across the tent. "So, start at the very beginning. Tell me absolutely everything!" he urged, the zeal in his voice betraying his attempts to appear calm.

"Your mother said you'd be the one to find them. I must admit, I was sceptical at first. Yet, here we are," he teased, a playful glint in his eyes. He glanced around the tent, as if addressing an imaginary audience that was silently captivated by his every word.

Before long, Luna told her Dad everything. She described vividly how she and Noah had spotted a tiny opening beneath a concealed ledge within the primary cave system. They had cleared away some shingle and soil, widening the gap until it allowed them to slip into an entirely new chamber. This chamber, which had been missed by all previous explorations of the cave system, was frozen.

But now they had finally discovered the hidden dinosaur eggs that the Appalachian legends talked about! According to the ancient lore, the Gods had left these eggs behind to aid humanity in the face of a cataclysmic threat to mankind in the future.

Her father listened intently, his fascination growing with every word. Luna had considered telling him about the eggs' mysterious faint glow that caught her eye when they first discovered them but decided to save that detail for another time. Maybe it was just a trick of the light, she thought. After all, the Professor preferred to deal in cold, hard facts. "Stick to the facts," he often advised, adding, "Most things are just points of view. I prefer things I can prove."

As soon as he had all the details from Luna, the Professor quickly got to work in the centre of his tent, his phone in hand and laptop on the rickety wooden table.

First, he hurriedly sent a flurry of emails to the heads of faculty at all the participating universities.

He then started to draw up plans for recovering the eggs from the cave.

Then finally, he gathered the core team together for a briefing on what Luna and Noah had discovered and how he thought best to carefully extract the eggs from the deep cave.

"We've found them, thousands of them!" he announced, adding, "Some of my team (as the Professor now referred to his daughter and Noah) have just arrived back. Apparently, the eggs are a long way in and there are thousands of them!"

"We will need to widen some passageways, by the sounds of it too", the Professor continued. "It sounds very narrow in places."

The Professor continued phoning and emailing all sorts of people, coordinating everything like a digital ninja.

"Yes, yes. Please get me a hundred more safety harnesses and climbing helmets, different sizes," the Professor demanded, his tone urgent and emphatic as he spoke into the phone. "And some rope too," he continued.

"We'll also require additional food and supplies for the extra workers needed to bring all these eggs to the surface," he continued, his determination evident.

"This is the discovery of the century," he yelled, getting quite animated now. "Find the funds, talk to the Head of Faculty at Kings," he asserted with resolve, referring to King's College, Cambridge.

Luna laughed at her father. She didn't really like it when he went into full boss mode. She preferred his soft, mischievous, and cheeky side. But he was in charge here and she guessed that sometimes he had to tell people what to do.

Soon, the sound of helicopter blades started to fill the sky with sound, bringing with them an influx of supplies, people, and extra equipment. Luna couldn't help but marvel at the organised chaos unfolding before her very eyes.

Extracting thousands of sizable, fossilised dinosaur eggs from deep inside of a mountain and navigating the intricate network of passageways connecting the vast caverns, pits, and open caves would indeed require meticulous planning and a lot of expertise.

After Noah and Luna had managed to snatch a few hours of sleep, the Professor roused them from their slumber. He asked them to guide some of the team back into the cave to show them the precise location of the dinosaur eggs.

"Rise and shine, you two sleepyheads," Professor Brown exclaimed. "We need you to lead us back to the eggs. I know you must be tired but needs must!"

"Once we pinpoint their exact location, the scientists and ground crew can work out how to move them outside safely," he continued. The Professor's eagerness to examine the eggs up close, conduct field tests, and begin the process of identification and cataloguing was obvious. "Rest can wait," he assured them, a mischievous chuckle escaping his lips.

Outside, a whirl of activity and enthusiasm enveloped the camp. Members of the team whispered excitedly, nudging each other, and pointing at Luna and Noah. One stout, bearded academic standing alongside another archaeologist, exclaimed, "That's them! Those are the kids who found them!"

"Yes. It's the Professor's daughter, Luna, and that friend of hers...I think he's called Noah, or something like that," replied another member of the team.

It seemed their fame was already spreading.

Luna smiled at Noah.

CHAPTER 3

The Hatching

F ast forward, to a point in time a couple of weeks later...

Almost all of the dinosaur eggs had now been recovered from the deep cave. It had proven to be a very big job and news of the discovery was starting to spread.

For the seventh time that morning, Professor Brown's eyes skimmed over the front page of The New York Herald, a broad smile lighting up his face. His second cup of Blue Mountain coffee that morning sat steaming beside a plate of his favourite beef sausages. He had saved those sausages for this very moment, though he had begun to doubt if he'd ever get the chance to enjoy them. As he savoured his breakfast, the sausages tasted better than ever - quite possibly the best he had ever eaten!

The Professor's appreciation for his meal was far from subtle, his vocal expressions of delight ringing out from his tent loudly. "Delicious! Absolutely divine!" he proclaimed loudly; his sense of accomplishment evident in his tone. As he savoured each bite, he mused aloud, "The sweet taste of success, no less." His words carried a touch of mild conceit, but Luna decided that he probably deserved his moment of glory, all things considered.

The local legend of hidden giant eggs had at times seemed more like a myth, even to the Professor. Yet, the recent discovery had turned doubt into reality, capturing the attention of the world's press in the process. As he devoured his meal and reflected on the recent turn of events, he couldn't help but feel that this moment might define his entire academic career once and for all. He even wondered if he might get a pay rise. With each sip of coffee and every satisfying bite of meaty sausage, he smiled broadly and continued to read and re-read the newspaper in front of him.

The front-page headline of his newspaper announced in big bold letters:

Dinosaur eggs discovered deep in the heart of the Appalachian Mountains!

The article continued, "Thousands of large dinosaur eggs have been discovered hidden deep in the Appalachian Mountains in Walker County, Northern Georgia. A team of scientists and environmentalists, led by Professor H. Brown of Cambridge University, found the eggs after a hunt reminiscent of a big Hollywood blockbuster film. Within a remote labyrinth of caves, a frozen cavern was found, housing a secret that has remained undiscovered for over sixty-six million years."

It had been almost three weeks since the initial discovery by Luna and Noah, and the Professor had managed to keep it relatively quiet up until now. But the world's media was beginning to wake up to the news and people around the globe were taking notice.

With his head held high and his chest puffed out, the Professor emerged from his tent, striding purposefully towards the mouth of the cave. The entrance was a hub of bustling activity, even though the sun had just begun to rise and cast its golden light upon the campsite.

Professor Brown's voice boomed through the air, a mix of urgency and excitement as he barked out orders, urging the team to "come on", "keep them coming" and "hurry up". Despite the early hour, the camp was alive with motion and energy. Luna and Noah stood nearby, watching the chaos before them, their laughter mingling with the commotion and noise.

Noah leaned towards Luna, his eyes twinkling, and said, "Thank goodness we insisted on coming!" Luna nodded in agreement, a big grin on her face. "I know," she chimed in, "Who knew we would be discovering ancient dinosaur eggs in the summer holidays?"

A human chain of explorers, cavers, and mountaineers had formed, carefully passing the dinosaur eggs from one to another. "Hold onto it tight," one advised the other, as they carefully handed over each egg. "They are heavier than they look."

Finally, the last of these hidden treasures of the frozen cavern were making their way into the light, ready to unveil their mysterious secrets.

One by one, the eggs continued to emerge from the mouth of the cave, carried carefully by the team members to a spacious, grassy area on the plateau. Here, they could be stored safely, awaiting the Professor's guidance on what needed to happen next. Luna and Noah stood captivated, their eyes following each egg's journey from the cave's entrance to the grassy plateau.

The eggs were placed in meticulous rows on the flat expanse of grass. Just a few hundred yards from the cave, the grassland was now adorned with hundreds of these limestone-clad, prehistoric relics. Positioned near the bustling tented kitchen that fed the camp, the flat ground provided an excellent makeshift sanctuary for the endless stream of dinosaur eggs that had been appearing above ground one by one, day after day.

Under the gentle warmth of the sun, the eggs glistened, their surfaces drying out and catching the light in a radiant display. Cracks and intricate patterns decorated their shells, telling the tale of their time in the hidden cavern. Small piles of prehistoric dust glinted, like fine diamonds, in the sun underneath each egg.

Luna couldn't help but notice that peculiar, light fluorescent purple glow that still seemed to continue to linger around the eggs, even in the daylight. It seemed to dance around the surface of each egg, sparkling and shimmering.

Eventually she mustered the courage to share this thought with her dad, the Professor, who swiftly dismissed the idea with a hearty scoff. "Minerals, my dear," he asserted with a touch of authority. "It's likely the minerals in the water that they sat in caused that. These eggs have been submerged in limestone and water for quite some time now. It's bound to happen. A classic case of mineralisation if you ask me."

Luna accepted his explanation. After all, her dad was a distinguished figure in the academic world while she was just a young schoolgirl, swept up in the adventure and excitement of it all. What did she know?

The eggs continued to emerge in a steady stream, like glistening treasure pulled from a hidden pirate ship. The workers toiled tirelessly, passing the eggs along the human chain like a relay team, strengthened by determination and teamwork. Some of their faces showed signs of exhaustion but their spirits remained unbroken. They pressed on, keen to get all the eggs out of the cave system as quickly as they possibly could.

Later that evening, as the sun dipped below the horizon, the camp transformed into a symphony of flickering lanterns and crackling campfires. Luna, Noah, and a few of their newfound friends and admirers gathered around a makeshift table to eat dinner together.

It was a Wednesday, so it was pizza night! The tantalising aroma of freshly baked pizza mingled with the crisp, clean mountain air. There was a choice of topping. Both Luna and Noah ordered American Hot - with extra pepperoni. It was their favourite.

Around them the camp was alive with activity. Conversations drifted through the air along with snippets of music, punctuated by bursts of laughter and the clinking of utensils. The hum of generators and the soft glow of lamps cast a warm and welcoming atmosphere, creating pockets of light in the jet-black darkness.

Noah and Luna chatted, enjoying the atmosphere and their new found fame.

"Hey Noah, do you remember that day we met at Harvard University when we were just young kids?" asked Luna.

"Of course, Luna! That was such an unforgettable day. Our parents were giving lectures, and there we were, two little explorers, meeting in the land of books and ideas," replied Noah.

"It's incredible how we instantly connected, right? I mean, I felt like I'd known you forever," said Luna, nodding.

Noah chuckled, "Yeah, it was like we had this secret bond from the very beginning. I knew we were destined to have some amazing adventures together."

"We've certainly had some great times together," Luna agreed excitedly. "Remember the time we decided to explore that cave near your campus? We had so much fun."

"How could I possibly forget? I thought that cave was like something out of a movie. We were like modern-day explorers, uncovering mysteries and treasure, even if it was just some cool rocks, fossils and crystals," agreed Noah, laughing.

As the group of young adventurers all sat eating pizza by the tented kitchen, they began hearing some strange, intermittent tapping noises coming from some of the eggs.

"It's probably just the eggs drying out," Luna ventured helpfully, her voice a nervous mix of mild excitement and uncertainty. Yet, even as she spoke, a sense of mystery and anticipation began to spread around the camp due to these strange tapping noises.

"It is peculiar," Noah agreed. "This hasn't happened before."

Then came a gentle and rhythmic constant beat, "tap, tap, tap, tickety, tap, tap, tap." Gradually, the melody was joined by other similar taps, growing in volume and rhythm. "Tippety, tappety, tic, toc, tic, toppety, tappety, tic, tac, toe, tap." The eggs continued to emit their own soft, magical Jurassic Morse code, a mysterious series of taps and rhythmic clicks. As the tapping noises harmonised, they swelled into a crescendo, weaving a rhythm that resembled rapid drumming, "Tipppety, tappetty, tic, toc, tippety, top tic top, toc."

Noah and Luna exchanged concerned glances, mirroring the expressions of the many site workers, cavers and scientists that sat around them. Most of them by now had halted their conversations. A hushed murmur swept through the groups. One voice rose above the rest, saying what everyone else was thinking, "What's that sound? Is it coming from the dinosaur eggs?"

More and more of the dinosaur eggs had joined this growing chorus of tapping, creating an eerie symphony, as if the eggs were engaged in some secret conversation with one another. And then, just as abruptly as it had begun, the tapping ceased, leaving a weighty silence in its wake.

Amid the quiet, Luna could hear a distant radio, playing a slightly off-key tune, its melodies floating across the camp. As her ears tuned in to it, she recognised the song, one of her favourite hip hop songs. Then, to her astonishment, the tapping resumed, perfectly synchronised with the rhythm of the song playing on the radio. The eggs also seemed to pulse light with a newfound intensity, their gentle rhythmic glow blending with the beat on the radio, growing brighter and more vibrant by the second.

Luna's eyes widened in amazement as she exchanged astonished glances with those around her. She summed up her excitement with a single loud "Wow!"

Professor Brown joined the crowd near the kitchen area, his curious eyes fixated on the unfolding spectacle, his head tilted to the side, once more like an inquisitive owl. With a thoughtful expression, he reached for the radio and started to change channels. As the sounds ceased and the flashing lights subsided, the Professor's owlish stare deepened, his brow furrowed in concentration. A faint, contemplative "hmmmmm", escaped his lips as he attempted to decipher the astonishing phenomenon that they were all witnessing.

With a bemused "hmmph," the Professor tuned the small radio to another channel. To everyone's astonishment, the tapping and radiant pulsating lights surged back to life, mirroring the rhythm of a new hip hop song that was now playing on the small radio with uncanny precision. The eggs seemed to almost come to life, playfully improvising with the melody, as if they were seasoned musicians jamming on stage. "Tackety, tippety, tappety, tic, toc, toc, tip, tip, tic, toppety, tappety, tic, tac, toe, toppety, tappety, tic," the eggs resonated to a pulsating beat.

The eggs' luminous display transformed the grassy plateau too, into a surreal disco dance floor, with throbbing lights casting vivid colours around the campsite.

Noah laughed and chimed in, "Seems we've got some egg-cellent DJs here in the house." Luna's laughter masked her surprise as she glanced at the incredible spectacle before her.

A mixture of excitement and trepidation swept across the Camp. The Professor moved towards one of the eggs to take a closer look, amazed at what was going on.

Then it happened!

A resounding "crack" shattered the air, as if the mountain behind them had split down the middle. The sound was soon joined by other sharp "cracks", a chorus of splitting noises and echoes reverberated through the camp: "click," "crack," "clack," and more. The ground trembled with each successive noise, like the rumble of a distant avalanche or the tumbling of huge rock fall down a cliff face. The eggs were starting to make a lot of noise, with a roar of explosive sound: "criiiiick," "clackkk," "crickkkk," "crunchhhhhhh," "clickkkkkkk-kkkkk," until it crescendoed into a thunderous"CliKKKKKKKKKKKKKKKKKKK-KKKKKKKKKKKKKKKKKKKKKKKClackKKKKKK!"

Before Luna, Noah, and their friends could fully comprehend what was happening, a crack appeared across one of the eggs close to them. They then watched the top of the egg fall off onto the grass. Slowly but surely, a small pink baby dinosaur, glistening with iridescent purple slime, climbed out onto the long, dry grass. The newborn dinosaur playfully rolled and wriggled on the grass, wiping off the bright luminous coating with which it was covered.

As if testing the newfound freedom of its legs, the young dinosaur wobbled upright, standing tall on its shaky, skinny limbs. In a comically high-pitched voice that matched its small stature well, it emitted an ear-piercing, squeaky roar, similar to a distressed kitten. "Reoooor," it called out, followed by a series of equally enthusiastic, albeit hilariously mismatched attempts at ever more fearsome roars: "Raaar," "Woooar," the young creature continued, its exuberance infectious.

Luna gasped as her eyes widened and she exchanged anxious glances with Noah and the Professor. "O.M.G.!!!" Noah slowly mouthed, his disbelief echoing through each letter.

Suddenly, the newly hatched dinosaur scurried over to Luna, captivated by her wide eyes and open mouth. The tiny creature tilted its head, studying her intently as if trying to understand her. It emitted a soft, low "purring" noise, full of curiosity: "Hurrrrrrr," "parrrrrr," "grrl."

Luna yelped. A tinge of fear crept into Luna's mind as she noticed its sharp teeth. What if the dinosaur was going to attack her? The realisation struck her that it might pose a threat even though the dinosaur was small.

"Hello, you beautiful baby dinosaur," she said in a gentle voice to the dinosaur, trying to remain calm.

Her worry soon gave way to a pleasant surprise.

In an unexpected turn of events, the dinosaur's attention shifted from Luna to her half-eaten pepperoni pizza and it swiftly snatched the pizza from her plate.

Before she knew it, the dinosaur had taken a big bite out of the uneaten pizza and was chewing it very carefully. It seemed like the young dinosaur was figuring what it tasted like, weighing up whether it actually liked pizza or not.

It let out a louder "Yeowlllllllllllllllll," resembling the howling of a noisy wild dog. The sound was so loud that the entire team of climbers and explorers looked to see what was happening, concerned for Luna and her safety.

"Are you OK, Luna?", shouted one of the younger scientists, in an alarmed voice, starting to get up out of his chair.

He ran towards Luna to see if he could help at all. In fact, quite a few of the team, including Luna's father, were now racing towards the unfolding drama at Luna's table.

Professor Brown attempted to take charge, shouting to everyone, "Come on, quickly."

The baby dinosaur then seemed to smile, looking around with the remaining pizza gripped tightly in his clawed hand. His eyes spotted a pile of large iridescent wood beetles on a rotten log. The dinosaur then quickly swiped the beetles onto the pizza, topping it off with some Tabasco sauce that had been sitting on a table nearby. The young pink dinosaur then promptly wolfed the whole thing down in a single mouthful. Its face gradually broke into a grin and before Luna and the others knew, it had started letting out some highly appreciative gurgling noises.

"Gurrrrggggh," cried the young dinosaur, letting out a second one in quick succession and then a third. Then the dinosaur just sat on the thick lush grass purring contentedly, like a cat that had just got the cream off the milk.

Luna wasn't sure about the cheese, pepperoni, and beetle toppings, or Tabasco sauce for that matter. In fact, she'd never even tasted Tabasco, and she certainly never had any intention of trying beetles on her pizza - ever! But hey, they are dinosaurs, she thought. What do you expect? Besides, at least he didn't want to eat her! What a relief, that could have been a disaster, thought Luna.

"Are you alright, my darling?", asked the Professor, seeming a little concerned and unsure what to do.

"I think so," answered Luna. "He seems to like pizza, of all things. I don't think he is dangerous. In fact, he seems quite friendly," she concluded.

The Professor watched the baby dinosaur closely, following its every move. A few of the team had arrived in a panic, carrying some rope and netting in case the dinosaur was dangerous and they needed to capture it quickly.

"Oh, I don't think there is any need for that," said the Professor knowingly. "It seems perfectly friendly to me," he said, more or less repeating what Luna had said to him a few moments earlier.

The newly hatched dinosaur looked like he might have some sort of half-formed pink feathers, very much like a young bird. But it was very hard to tell exactly, as is often the case with newborn creatures. His faintly coloured orange eyes that sported just a glimmer of green around them seemed utterly transfixed and full of love for Luna.

Quite why this was the case was difficult to say. Maybe it was because she was the one that had discovered their eggs deep in the cave. Or perhaps it was just that she had a tasty pizza ready to hand that the young hungry dinosaur could easily snatch and eat as its first meal.

Professor Brown was soon proclaiming loudly that, "Often with birds, when they first hatch, the first creature they see they believe is their mother and they often then copy her behaviour."

"It's how they survive in the wild," he continued. "And this chap looks like he is a flying dinosaur of some kind!"

"I've seen ducks who live with people, watch TV with them and climb into the washing-up to help try to clean the dishes," he rambled on.

"Perfectly normal," the Professor concluded emphatically. "Perfectly normal. Just what you would expect."

Luna raised her eyebrows. As far as she could see there was nothing "perfectly normal" about any of this and this certainly wasn't a duck!

Soon after, a bunch of other baby dinosaurs started to hatch and were gathering around Luna, making all sorts of wild noises - yelping, howling, purring, and gurgling. They really were quite a noisy bunch. And very demanding.

The Professor and some of his team stood by, watching closely what was going on, making sure Luna and Noah were safe.

"Well, well, what do we have here?" Professor Brown shouted over the noise, trying to take charge again and attempting to engage some of the hatching dinosaurs directly. But the baby dinosaurs simply ignored him, much to his disappointment. Their eyes were focused solely on Luna and Noah, as they continued to make their noisy racket enthusiastically in the direction of the two young intrepid explorers.

In no time at all, Luna had become something of a dino superstar. More and more of the little critters hatched and started to demand fresh pizza from her. Before she knew it, a big group of them were surrounding her, all desperate for pizza. The kitchen was having to make a lot of pizzas very quickly, carrying them out to Luna's table in a constant stream. The dinosaurs were making a real ruckus as they howled and yowled for pizza.

Luna held her breath, hoping the kitchen had enough pizza dough to feed all the dinosaurs. The baby dinosaurs were very hungry and it seemed like pizza was exactly what they wanted to eat. They jostled with one another, trying to be first to grab a piece of pizza.

"Hey, little ones! I've got more yummy pizza for you here," Luna called to each baby dinosaur as they hatched. They were all very excited and completely ravenous, grabbing more and more pizza from Luna's hands. She could hardly keep up.

"Steady now," "Hey, take it easy!" "Wait your turn!" Luna shouted, getting increasingly frustrated with their bad table manners.

"Sooooooo rude," she shouted at one of them.

The dinosaurs obviously had very strange tastes when it came to pizza toppings. They insisted on adding all sorts of unusual foods from other people's plates and tables to their pizza. There were some half-eaten pieces of fish, peanut butter, custard, tomato ketchup, a squashed moth or two, canned tomatoes, some sand flies, a giant grasshopper and even some hazelnut spread for good measure.

Luna had to tell a couple of the baby dinosaurs to calm down because they were getting far too excited and were grabbing hold of anything to top their pizzas with. They tried paper napkins, toothpicks and even a glass pepper pot.

"That's not really a very good idea," Luna said emphatically to a newly hatched dinosaur with strange webbed feet, prising a bunch of flowers from its grasp.

Then Luna finally put her foot down when one of them tried to add cigarette butts to their pizza from an unattended ashtray. "No, no, no, no, no!" Luna cried.

At that moment, Noah swiftly grabbed the ashtray from the dinosaurs, hiding it from their view. Enough was enough!

"They're really quite crazy, you know," Noah exclaimed, raising his voice above the relentless dinosaur squawks, yelps and howls.

"And they really seem to like you," Noah added, trying to be heard above the noise.

Professor Brown just shook his head, amazed and slightly jealous of all the attention Luna was getting. Though he couldn't help but smile at his daughter with a degree of fatherly pride.

Over the next few hours, Luna, Noah, and some of their friends got the dinosaurs to try all sorts of pizza toppings. Noah attempted to feed one of them some sardines on a wholemeal pizza base with no cheese at all. "Here, try this. It's sardine. They are very good for you and I've covered them in a delicious tomato sauce for you," he told the excited young dinosaur who just spat it out across the field.

"Well, that didn't go down too well at all, did it?", Noah said laughing.

"I think it's because you didn't top it with cheese," suggested Luna.

"Or maybe they just don't like wholemeal pizza?" Noah mused. "I know I don't!"

"Or maybe they don't like sardines," they both chimed together.

"Well, they are disgusting," concluded Noah. "I hate them."

"Mind you, I'm not sure I much like any of their special toppings to be quite honest," said Luna emphatically.

It wasn't until four in the morning that the campsite chefs had managed to make enough pizza to satisfy the hunger of hundreds, maybe even thousands, of newly hatched baby dinosaurs.

Most of the eggs that had been brought out of the cave in the first week had hatched but some remained unhatched.

Professor Brown had a serious talk with the Head Chef, saying, "You're going to need to get a lot more pizza dough over the next few days. And don't forget the Mozzarella cheese and tomatoes! Maybe buy a whole load of other tinned ingredients too while we work out what they really like to eat. It's clear they have very different tastes from us."

"They seem to like all sorts, Sir," the Head Chef replied. "I'll get a lot of different options so we can work out precisely what they will eat."

The Professor nodded and "snorted" his agreement.

Once all the hatched dinosaurs were fed, Luna and Noah lay on the grass, staring at the stars, utterly worn out.

"What a day, huh?" Noah sighed.

Luna agreed, feeling the grass vibrate underneath her with a loud, contented "Purrrrrrrrrrrrrrrrrrr." Three of the first dinosaurs to hatch lay next to them, gazing up at the sky, purring happily together. The ground gently vibrating, the crickets and grasshoppers chirping all around.

Getting to Know the Dinosaurs

Luna and Noah were truly astonished by the wild and outlandish pizza toppings that the dinosaurs came up with and ate. When it came to pizza toppings, their creativity knew no bounds.

There were combinations like sake and clams with prune sauce; black squid and wasabi; fried leeks with peanut butter and pumpkin; and beetroot with mustard and custard.

Luna talked to the dinosaurs as if they were her own young children, encouraging them to try new things to eat and getting them to explore the camp site and surrounding mountains.

"Come on," she said to one of them. "Strawberry trifle is delicious. Try it."

She soon discovered though that they were naturally very curious and somehow often just worked things out for themselves.

Many of the unusual pizza toppings the dinosaurs liked weren't something a human would ever consider eating but they did the trick in satisfying the dinosaurs' hunger.

The ever-increasing amounts of pizza they ate ensured the young dinosaurs grew rapidly.

Even though the dinosaurs were still very young, Luna's suspicions that there were three distinct types of dinosaurs were confirmed.

The first dinosaur to hatch, which Luna had decided to call Oscar, had something resembling rough, short, crumpled up wings. They had begun to open up and before long, short pink feathers were starting to sprout everywhere.

"He's my favourite," Luna told Noah. "I know I shouldn't have favourites but I do. I just like him best. There is something special about him."

"I like these other two that are always following him around as well...almost as much", conceded Luna, hugging all three of them lovingly.

One of the other two dinosaurs that followed Oscar had gills and was more at home in the streams and lakes around the camp. Luna suspected that she was a female. She called this one Astrid.

Astrid was an amazing swimmer and could swim underwater for long periods of time in the lake that was nearby, set high in the thick pine forest to the right of the camp site. She had scared Luna a few times though by disappearing for over ten minutes at a time under the dark crystal water of the lake. It was very deep in places.

Luna would shout frantically at the surface of the lake, "Astrid, Astrid, are you OK? Astrid?". Then all of a sudden, Astrid would reappear in a big splash and squirt a huge plume of water from her mouth, completely soaking Luna in the process.

But after a few scares it was fairly obvious that Astrid was an excellent swimmer and could easily stay underwater for hours at a time.

The third and final dinosaur in this close group, resembled the typical land dinosaurs Luna had read about in books and seen in pictures when she was a young child, visiting museums with her father. She named this dinosaur Alexander.

Alexander was very handsome. His scales were red, turquoise and orange. His eyes a striking dark green. But even he didn't quite hold the same special place in Luna's heart that Oscar did.

Oscar soon learnt how to open cans and jars of food and was trying his own combinations of pizza toppings and the other dinosaurs seemed to copy him. Whatever he did, they did.

Oscar liked to build things out of scrap wood and other materials that had been thrown out by members of the team at the campsite. He never seemed to want to waste a thing.

The Professor was always very impressed by Oscar's building exploits. He was forever saying to Oscar, "Good lad, that's it, keep upcycling all our rubbish!"

Oscar made the most intricate and impressive camp sites out of old sheets of cardboard, string, and wooden planks for Astrid, Alexander and him to shelter in. One of these was modelled on the Taj Mahal, after Oscar had seen it on a postcard that had arrived for Noah. Oscar could create the most amazing things out of rubbish that most people would simply just throw away.

He also seemed to be the leader of the dinosaurs and Luna got the impression that the dinosaurs had a kind of shared consciousness. Once Oscar mastered something, all the others seemed to do so as well, almost automatically. As they grew, so did their capabilities and knowledge - in huge leaps and bounds.

The dinosaurs simply adored Luna. It was as if they knew that she was the one who found them deep in the mountain. Everywhere Luna went, they followed.

One day, as Luna and her dad observed their bustling activity in the camp, Luna couldn't help but share her thoughts about the dinosaurs' astonishing progress with him.

"Dad, have you noticed how quickly the dinosaurs are learning?" she said.

"Yes. Oscar's a marvel with his building projects," Professor Brown agreed.

"No, it's more than that, Dad. It's like they are all connected somehow."

"Connected? How do you mean connected, darling?" The Professor asked.

"Well, whenever Oscar learns something new, it's like the others pick it up almost instantly. Even if they aren't there. It's not just about mimicking; it's like they have some sort of shared consciousness. I can't explain it exactly."

Her dad raised an eyebrow, intrigued by Luna's observation.

"Shared consciousness? Now that's quite an idea, he concluded.

"I know it sounds wild, but watch this," said Luna.

Luna then called out to Oscar, who was currently engrossed in constructing an elaborate new structure from some discarded materials.

"Oscar, can you show us what you've just worked out, without letting the other dinosaurs see you do it?", asked Luna.

Oscar nodded and demonstrated a complex series of new woodworking techniques with the materials he had been using, something that he had only just learned.

To Luna's delight, the other dinosaurs, Astrid and Alexander included, then started to do exactly what Oscar had just done.

Professor Brown was astonished. "That's remarkable," he said. "It's like they're all tapped into the same learning network."

"Right? It's not just about individual learning. It's like they have a collective intelligence of some sort," confirmed Luna.

Professor smiled broadly. "If that's the case, Luna, it would explain why their knowledge grows so quickly."

"They're super smart, Dad." said Luna proudly, as if she were boasting about her own children's abilities.

As Luna spoke, several dinosaurs gathered around her, their eyes gleaming with a sense of connection and understanding.

The professor chuckled. "Well, it seems you've made quite a discovery, Luna. A bunch of genius dinosaurs with a shared consciousness, eh?" he said.

"It's really amazing, Dad," Luna said, as she grinned widely.

Professor Brown nodded, realising that their unconventional family of dinosaurs held more mysteries than he had initially thought.

Noah then arrived, out of the blue.

"You are a bit like the Pied Piper, they follow you everywhere," he joked.

It was true, they never left Luna alone.

They would jump up and playfully lick her face, despite Luna's protests. She'd tell them to "Get down," "No, don't do that," and "Stop licking my face!". Noah would just laugh.

"Well, they sure love you, dude," Noah remarked. "What are they gonna do when you have to go back home to England?".

Luna tried really hard not to think about that, wishing that this summer could just go on forever. Many girls her age might not have enjoyed all this attention and responsibility but Luna absolutely loved it!

Before long, a small group of two journalists and two photographers were let into the camp by the Professor, to "take a look" at the rapidly growing dinosaurs – for an "exclusive scoop", as he referred to it.

The Professor had agreed to let them see the dinosaurs for themselves. He also had allowed them to interview him and take a few photographs of Luna and Noah with the dinosaurs. But he insisted on no film of the dinosaurs as they could be quite boisterous. He didn't want members of the public panicking about wild dinosaurs rampaging around the countryside. He hoped that allowing a select group of journalists in for an exclusive photo opportunity would satisfy the media's hunger for news - for the time being anyway.

"So, tell me all about your dinosaurs then, Luna," asked a dark-haired lady journalist, with a smart woollen dark suit, expensive looking gold jewellery and a slight Italian accent. "What did you think at first when they all hatched?" Her name was Daniella and she was aged about 45, Luna guessed. About the same age as Luna's mother.

"Well, Noah and I were very surprised when we found the eggs deep in the cave and even more amazed when the eggs started to hatch. Since then, we've been getting to know the dinosaurs better - watching them grow and develop, particularly these three."

"Can you communicate with them at all? Do you think they can understand you?" Daniella asked.

"Well, I keep talking to them and they certainly seem to be learning, very quickly in fact," Luna explained. "I don't suppose they will ever be able to talk though. They just yelp, howl and purr," Luna said.

As the interview continued, Oscar took an interest in the laptop the other journalist had set up on a picnic table.

The young male journalist it belonged to was called James. He had been showing Oscar how it worked and how you could search for things online. Oscar had watched intently and looked genuinely interested in this.

Once James had moved away from the laptop computer and left it unsupervised Oscar just started poking away at the keys. Slowly to start with and then very quickly.

James yelled at Oscar, more out of concern that his laptop might get broken than anything else, "Hey, Oscar, stop that, leave my laptop alone... Oscar, please stop."

Oscar completely ignored him and kept tapping away at the keyboard frantically. He was surprisingly deft at typing for a dinosaur and he seemed to know what he was doing.

The journalist stood behind Oscar to see what he was doing exactly and to see if he could safely wrestle the pink feathered dinosaur away from his computer.

"Oh my gosh," said the young journalist, laughing. "He's searching for 'unusual, wild foraged, pizza toppings'."

Sure enough, it was true. Oscar had very quickly worked out how to search for things on the Internet. As his keyboard skills improved minute by minute, he was searching for all sorts of things on James's laptop.

Luna and Noah laughed. None of the team who were working as part of the camp would be at all surprised. They knew all too well how super smart the dinosaurs were but the journalists were completely dumbfounded.

Oscar searched and read things on the screen of the laptop rapidly. He worked at what seemed like hypersonic speed and before long Astrid and Alexander came and watched what Oscar was doing too. It seemed impossible that anyone could search, then read and digest so much information as quickly as Oscar could.

Oscar then started to look at video footage of one of the most famous and popular hip hop artists, turning the sound on the computer up. His foot was soon tapping on the ground, his head bobbing, and he started to purr again. Oscar was in his element!

"They sure do dig hip hop," said Noah to the journalists.

Astrid and Alexander joined in too and started to dance behind Oscar. They were all purring together, moving and grooving to the sounds coming from the computer.

James had bookmarked a news channel's website where Oscar found a teenage Swedish girl talking in a highly animated manner about climate change. At this point he slowed down how quickly he was reading and really started to concentrate on the messages featured in this blog. He was clearly reading every word very carefully and thinking about what it meant. He seemed to actually look serious for the first time. And then the purring stopped.

Oscar clicked on a series of links in the blog and opened up other online articles and videos. One showed how coral reefs were being decimated and rainforests were being flattened. Another explained how countries like Bangladesh, Pakistan and Indonesia were getting terribly flooded and how this was affecting their populations. As he read, he seemed to become more and more subdued. Luna thought she could see a small tear in the corner of Oscar's right eye.

Oscar then encouraged the other two dinosaurs to have a go on the laptop too. Sure enough, they were able to operate it just as well as Oscar almost immediately. What Oscar had learnt, they had learnt.

They soon switched back to watching videos of hip hop artists, online games, people playing basketball and cooking programmes about how to make the perfect pizza. This seemed to cheer the other dinosaurs back up, although Oscar never seemed quite the same after his deep dive into climate change.

The two journalists were utterly transfixed by this activity. They had never seen anything quite like it. But then again, they had never met a trio of super smart dinosaurs before either.

CHAPTER 5

Oscar Starts to Speak

The weeks went by and all the dinosaurs were now hatched. So far, Professor Brown had managed to keep media coverage of the dinosaurs to a minimum. But it was clear that this couldn't last forever.

Professor Brown gazed up into the spring sky, watching a group of helicopters circling, like a swarm of irate wasps. The whole situation was turning into quite a spectacle. With a loud "Phut!", the Professor exhaled a loud puff of breath into the increasingly noisy sky. Not that he minded his name and photo being splashed across nearly every big newspaper and global TV channel. In fact, he felt really quite thrilled! He was particularly pleased that the media had used a picture of him when he was a lot younger, from the university's website.

"Well, it seems the press has really started to arrive in force now," Professor Brown remarked in a slightly agitated voice - even though he loved every minute of it really.

Thankfully, the media couldn't easily drive their trucks in any large numbers close to the campsite because the National Guard had blocked the road. So for now, they could keep most of the media at a distance from the actual campsite.

"We can't keep the media from poking around indefinitely," the Professor grumbled to anyone who cared to listen. "They can be quite a nuisance. Nothing seems off limits to them," he added knowingly. "That's why I let my two pet journalists in here. In the hope we could keep the devils at bay until our work is complete."

Unfortunately though, TV cameras from a Swiss TV channel in one of the circling helicopters had already filmed about 50 dinosaurs frolicking and playing on the grassy plateau together and the footage of this had been instantly broadcasted around the world. The news was spreading like wildfire. The world was becoming more and more aware of the dinosaurs and the appetite for more news about them was increasing by the minute.

The Professor had also just been informed that the President of the United States was planning to visit the campsite to "take a look" at the dinosaurs and was intending to address the nation live about this incredible discovery. Really, the president wanted to assess the situation first hand. There were discussions in certain circles that these dinosaurs might pose a potential threat to national security or even to the general public. Farmers were already lobbying the White House, asking if the government could guarantee the safety of their livestock. And one large pizza chain had already imposed a ban on dinosaurs eating in their restaurants as a publicity stunt. All their branches had enormous posters in the windows that read 'NO DINOSAURS ALLOWED.'

The dinosaurs were growing at an astonishing rate, fuelled by a diet of pizza – topped with all the crazy extras they loved. And now they even knew how to use computers! Oscar and his friends continued to play online games, listen to hip hop music, and trawl the internet for new ideas.

When they were thirsty, they mostly drank water from a nearby stream. However, some of them had begun occasionally sipping from cans of cola. This did tend to make them burp quite loudly and when they did so, they burped with a proud and somewhat dramatic series of bowing gestures. They seemed to treat burping as a form of formal greeting to one another.

The dinosaurs also continued to develop an ever increasing liking for hip-hop and rap music. They often borrowed the camp radio, until a young environmentalist on the Professor's team showed them how to download music using an old laptop computer which he gave to Oscar as a gift. After that, there was no stopping their musical exploits, with masses of them dancing and bobbing around to their favourite sounds.

Luna checked their browsing history to see exactly what they had been looking at. She soon discovered that Oscar and his dinosaur buddies were spending hours scouring the Internet for anything and everything, from fashion trends to saving the planet, from unravelling the mysteries of nuclear fission to cooking up an eco-friendly pizza recipe. They soaked up knowledge like sponges and would have outshone even the brightest high school whizz kid.

The dinosaurs spent a fair amount of time playing online games and they had started to excel at these too. Oscar and another smaller bird-like dinosaur by the name of Orinoco were already topping multiple global gaming leaderboards.

Online gamers around the world, from Alaska to Australia, from the Philippines to Peru, would be amazed to learn that they were being beaten by a pair of crazy, pizza eating, dinosaur gamers who weren't even three months old!

One day Luna came up behind Astrid while she was on the computer, only to discover she had over 50 tabs open, each one relating to plastic pollution in the world's oceans.

Another afternoon, Noah giggled and nudged Luna, saying, "Hey, Oscar has started doing a load of online language courses now."

Luna raised an eyebrow in surprise. "Language courses? Seriously? They can't even talk!" she laughed. "Who knows what's going on in their crazy dino minds? They're online non-stop," she joked.

It was true. A couple of the dinosaurs, including Oscar, had dived into language courses, binge-listening to lessons in every tongue known to humanity - from Arabic to Zulu.

Despite their newfound digital prowess, the dinosaurs still hadn't spoken a word or found a clear way to communicate with Luna or the other humans. They just exchanged a few quizzical looks here and there, uttered the occasional purr and a theatrical burp now and then.

The dinosaurs dedicated a lot of time to observing human activities but their number one obsession seemed to be vehicles. The cars, trucks, and helicopters that arrived at the campsite drew their attention like bees to honey. They sniffed exhaust pipes, popped open petrol caps to peer inside and exchanged knowing glances between one another as they did so.

Oscar in particular seemed unhappy by the presence of cars, trucks and buses, emitting disapproving grunts and the occasional mournful howl.

Luna, sensing his distress, asked him, "Oscar, what's wrong? Are you upset about the cars?" But Oscar, though appearing sad, remained silent, his head hanging low.

Luna shared her observation with Noah, "You know, Oscar seems really bothered by cars. He's almost fixated on them. I swear I saw him looking sad in the parking lot."

Noah chuckled, "Maybe they want to take driving lessons but can't get a licence?"

Luna gave a sigh, responding, "Well, that's not very helpful, Noah. They just seem to dislike cars and petrol fumes."

Noah shrugged, offering, "Who knows? They seem pretty happy about driving and flying when they are playing online games."

The dinosaurs' personalities began to take shape as Luna and Noah spent more and more time with them. Among the group, Oscar stood out as the playful, inventive ringleader. His eyes sparkled with curiosity and often came up with some amazing solutions to the challenges he encountered.

He had a protective and nurturing nature, always looking out for the other dinosaurs, guiding them with wisdom beyond his years (well in his case, weeks). He had a habit of tilting his head to one side too - a gesture that seemed to emphasise his obvious cleverness.

Oscar was also regularly joined by another beautiful feathered dinosaur that Luna named Hugo.

Hugo was very gentle and thoughtful and Oscar seemed to like him a lot. Luna wondered if he was Oscar's brother. They seemed very close.

Hugo had beautiful golden feathers that shimmered in the sunlight. His eyes were a gorgeous pink with a turquoise surround. He also had a beautiful turquoise snout. He didn't join Oscar every day but he was a regular visitor. He was much quieter and gentler than Oscar. Often just watching, listening and observing.

Luna wished that the dinosaurs could talk. To make up for their inability to speak, she spent hours and hours teaching them about everything that she thought they might find interesting. She pointed out the birds and animals that lived in and around the camp and explained about the weather and the sun and the moon.

But then, just as Luna had almost given up any hope of ever being able to talk with the dinosaurs, something rather remarkable happened. Oscar began to speak directly to Luna. Startled, Luna sat glued to her chair, spilling her fruit juice onto her jeans as she stared with wide open eyes at Oscar.

Oscar gazed into Luna's eyes as he softly stuttered and stumbled over his words. "Thanking you verily much dude for discovering us, our dear, darling Loooonarrr. You are our very best friend." "We love you very much, dude," he purred with affection, his eyes shining with warmth.

He spoke in a way that mixed up very old-fashioned, formal English with street jargon and the occasionally completely unacceptable word or profanity. Luna guessed that he had picked these up from the hip hop and rap songs that the dinosaurs loved so much.

"I didn't think you could talk or understand what I was saying to you," Luna replied.

"We can understand you Looonaar, we are learning English, yo Loony!" came Oscar's response. "But we communicates using our minds. We are teleportic!" he added.

"I think you might mean telepathic", Luna corrected him.

"Yes", agreed Oscar quickly.

"And now that we are talking to each other, please never, and I mean never, refer to me or anyone else, as 'Yo Loony'! It is very rude," Luna told Oscar.

"I am verily sorry Looonaaar. We heard it on the radio. And it sounds like Loonaar," replied Oscar, sounding suitably told off.

"Alright Oscar. I accept your apology. Looks like I'll have to give you and your friends some speedy English lessons," Luna said, now feeling guilty for telling him off quite so abruptly.

"Why do you call me Oscar?" asked Oscar.

"I just thought you should have a name," Luna replied patiently. "And I thought it was a nice name that suited you," she continued.

"I already have a very ancient dinosaur name though, we all do," said Oscar. "Mine is Almanza, Backseat Driver, Afterglow, Miami Ink, Maverick, Sabre, Collooney, Tartan Tease" Oscar told Luna with a very serious face.

"You are kidding me, right?" replied Luna, trying hard not to laugh.

Oscar paused, then after a few moments of straight-faced silence, a broad grin spread across his face. "Yes! It is just jokes! I got those names from an internet site about pedigree dogs." My name is some high-pitched noises you humans can't even hear. So let's stick with Oscar! I like it!" he replied.

Luna playfully shook her head at Oscar, feigning exasperation. "Oh, Oscar, what am I going to do with you?" she said with a chuckle.

So from then on, she took on the role of being Oscar's personal English tutor, patiently teaching him the proper way to speak and highlighting what was considered rude, obscene, or completely unacceptable.

Before long, Oscar was asking Luna a lot of questions. "Why do you humans use that petrol in all your cars? It is poisoning the Earth you know. You will end up extinct like us dinosooors did 66 millions of years ago if you aren't too careful," Oscar stumbled and stuttered over his words, as he slowly learnt how to speak and pronounce things properly.

"That's why I get upsets when I looks at cars and helicopters. There has to be a better way for you to travel and go on your holidays and make your houses warm?" pleaded Oscar.

Luna nodded in agreement and explained to Oscar, "Many people think the same way, Oscar. However, it's very difficult to completely move away from our dependence on fossil fuels."

"Us dinosooors wants to help you humans. We have got a few ideas about better ways to do these things," Oscar stated emphatically. "Most of the answers are on the internet," he continued enthusiastically. "We loves the internet, it is sick dude!"

"I never would have guessed that you like the internet...er dude," laughed Luna.

After a pause, Luna took a moment to explain to Oscar that the President of the United States would be visiting in the next few days, accompanied by the world's media. She emphasised the importance of good behaviour and avoiding any actions that might be seen as scary or dangerous. Luna shared her concern that they could all end up in zoos or safari parks if they didn't act sensibly.

Oscar just laughed and reassured Luna, saying, "No stress dude. If that happens, we will just disappear." He winked as he said this.

Curious and puzzled, Luna asked, "What do you mean by 'just disappear'?" And then, with a loud pop Oscar suddenly just vanished into thin air, leaving Luna completely bewildered and alarmed. She frantically searched for him everywhere. She looked in her tent, under a big truck, behind several other tents, calling out for him, worried about how she would explain his sudden disappearance to her father, the Professor. "Oscar! Oscar!", she shouted. "This isn't funny, please stop this! Come out! Pleeease! Oscar! Where are you?"

With another loud pop, Oscar reappeared, wearing a mischievous grin. "We can go vin-isible," he playfully declared.

A mixture of both relief and exasperation was clearly evident as Luna scolded him, "You scared me half to death! Please don't ever do that again! And by the way, it is invisible...not vinisible."

"Whatever," scoffed Oscar flippantly.

Luna continued their English lesson, while pondering whether she should inform the professor about Oscar's newfound ability to disappear. Ultimately, she decided to keep his disappearing act a secret, at least for the time being. After all, the Professor would have enough to process with Oscar's sudden ability to speak.

Oscar's English skills improved rapidly as they shared a large pizza that afternoon. Despite a few amusing and basic mistakes, he absorbed everything incredibly rapidly.

Luna found herself giggling to herself. It was like teaching a toddler to speak who understood complex concepts like splitting the atom and solar flares.

As this first formal English lesson ended, Luna explained to Oscar that she couldn't possibly teach all the dinosaurs individually. It would simply take far too long! Oscar reassured her, saying, "It is OK Loonaar. We are telepathic. When you teach me, you teach us all at the same time. We are more advanced than you humans." His English was clearly progressing fast, though Luna couldn't believe for a minute that dinosaurs were more advanced than humans.

"I thought that you had some sort of shared consciousness or something," Said Luna. "My dad and I had noticed that if one of you learns something you all do."

"Yes," agreed Oscar emphatically.

Oscar ran off towards some of the other dinosaurs, including Alexander and Hugo. They were eager to talk about everything they had learned through Oscar's lesson with Luna.

They raced up the hill - their figures outlined against the brilliant ice-blue sky - and then with a pop they all vanished completely. Luna couldn't help but sigh; this disappearing business was going to be a problem.

CHAPTER 6

The President is Coming

For a few days before the President arrived the camp was a hive of activity, with Secret Service men and women checking everything to make sure it was safe for the President. They gave Oscar and his friends a very close once over to check they weren't dangerous and that they didn't bite!

Oscar asked one of the Secret Service men, "Are you FBI or CIA?" The Secret Service man just stared and said nothing.

Then one of the female agents said, "We are Homeland Security", not quite believing she was actually talking to a dinosaur.

There was a team setting up a big marquee as well as a stage on the edge of the grassy plateau. They spent hours making sure everything was perfect. Several army snipers with rifles set up in the mountains overlooking the entire area to make sure that the President would be safe once he arrived.

Before they knew it, the big day arrived. The sky was painted with dark streaks of smoke and wispy clouds, heavy with an endless stream of helicopters. The President and by implication the world's media were on their way.

However, there was not a trace of the dinosaurs. Not a single one remained. The only evidence of their existence were the shattered limestone egg fragments scattered across the flat grass area near the camp.

Professor Brown was in a state of panic, "We can't just lose thousands of dinosaurs, each the size of a large dog or a small horse!" he exclaimed almost tearfully, his voice tinged with desperation.

"Search the camp thoroughly. They can't have just disappeared. Could they have returned to their cave, do you think? Has anyone checked it? The President will be here soon! What will we tell him if we can't find them?" he said desperately.

Luna and Noah exchanged uncertain glances, their shoulders rising in a helpless shrug. The Professor let out an exasperated sigh, his frustration evident as he stormed off toward the main cave entrance to check for himself.

Throughout the morning there was still no sign of the dinosaurs. However, a lot of pizza dough had mysteriously vanished overnight, along with 200 cans of prunes, 100 cans of clam chowder, and a huge quantity of cheese. The large container that held the custard powder seemed to have gone down dramatically too.

The Professor paced back and forth, audibly huffing and puffing in distress. Luna worried her Dad might have a heart attack if they didn't find the dinosaurs soon.

And then, as if by magic, three of the dinosaurs materialised out of thin air with a resounding pop! It was Oscar, accompanied by Alexander and Astrid.

Relieved, Luna managed to compose herself and uttered, "Thank goodness you've returned." Noah chimed in too with a nervous "Phew!" and raised his eyebrows in a mixture of relief and mild alarm.

"We are here, Mr Professor, Sir, to meet Mr President, Him's Majesty, King of the United Taters, Prince of the Northern Mericas. We have been elected by the other dinosaurs to say hello to him," Oscar proclaimed in a surprisingly eloquent and professional tone.

Luna couldn't help but notice that Oscar looked particularly polished today, as if he had cleaned himself up and brushed his feathers for the occasion. Alexander and Astrid also appeared to have put extra effort into their appearance, standing with a sense of purpose and determination.

With clear irritation, Professor Brown asked Oscar, "Where are the other dinosaurs?"

Oscar promptly responded, "The others are waiting to see what happens." He then muttered something about his friends not wanting to end up in a zoo, or a cage, or a Jurassic theme park.

Luna blushed. She realised that she might have sown the seeds of the zoo idea in Oscar's mind, which in turn seemed to have spread panic throughout the rest of the dinosaurs.

Meanwhile, the Professor was worried about the credibility of his astonishing discovery. He fretted that the President might doubt the authenticity of the thousands of dinosaur eggs found in the cave. Nevertheless, the fact that the eggs had hatched and three of the dinosaurs were now speaking and even meeting the President would hopefully provide enough evidence to prove that this large horde of dinosaurs did actually exist.

The President's official helicopter, Marine One, emerged over a nearby mountain, flanked by two smaller, heavily-armed military helicopters. Their synchronised rotor blades created a rhythmic "thwack-a-thwack-a-thwack-a-thwack-a-thwack-a-thwack-a," as they drew closer. With precision they touched down on the long expanse of green grass beside the scattered remains of the cracked eggshells.

A stream of other helicopters followed one after another, with CNN, Fox News, SKY, BBC and Reuters printed on their sides. The dinosaurs had become a major news story around the globe and the world's media was clearly going to feast on every bit of it. The fact that the dinosaurs could speak wouldn't be a secret for much longer, the Professor thought.

Before long, the President strode confidently out of his helicopter toward a temporary stage, accompanied by a horde of Secret Service men and women in sharp suits and dark glasses. The stage was adorned with flimsy strings of bunting, a big Stars and Stripes flag, and a wooden podium bearing the President's Seal of Office on its front.

One of the Secret Service men gently tapped the microphone to check if it worked, saying "Testing, testing," before introducing the President. "Ladies and gentlemen, please stand for the President of the United States," he announced.

Everyone who had been seated immediately sprung to their feet and a few people clapped enthusiastically, including Oscar. However, Luna doubted if Oscar truly understood why he was applauding.

The President stood behind the podium and delivered a speech to welcome the dinosaurs, offering compliments to the professor and his team. He was dressed in a very sharp, dark, and expensive-looking suit, along with a slim, dark tie. Everything about him appeared immaculate. His black shoes shone like mirrors. However, he was smaller in stature than Luna had imagined.

The President spoke enthusiastically, saying "Ladies and Gentlemen, this a genuinely historic moment, a ground-breaking discovery, the first stage in understanding what really happened to the dinosaurs millions of years ago and an opportunity to know more about why mankind is superior in every way to all other life forms on Earth." He hardly paused for breath.

Luna observed with a mix of amusement and concern as Oscar and his friends, Astrid and Alexander, found the President's comments about mankind being superior utterly hilarious. They giggled uncontrollably, not bothering to conceal how funny they found it.

Oscar, not being able to contain himself, asked in a hushed tone, "Is he always this funny? He's completely jokes dude. Lol!" Luna gestured for Oscar to lower his voice and informed him that the President was being serious.

The moment had arrived for the President to meet the dinosaurs. The Secret Service agents surrounding him appeared visibly jittery and tense. Despite their imposing and muscular stature, their hands gripped the concealed weapons beneath their jackets tightly.

Each agent wore small earphones and miniature microphones were clipped discreetly to their clothing, enabling them to communicate in hushed voices. For this particular occasion, they had designated the President the codename 'T-Rex,' a detail that even Luna found amusing.

It became apparent that the Secret Service agents were not entirely sure how to approach the task of protecting the President from a trio of large juvenile dinosaurs. Their hands were on their guns constantly, ready for trouble, as Luna, The Professor and two young scientists walked up onto the stage towards the podium with the three dinosaurs behind them. The agents exchanged cautious glances, trying to anticipate any unpredictable moves from the dinosaurs while maintaining an air of readiness for whatever might unfold.

The Professor wore his favourite brown tweed jacket and trousers while the scientists donned bright, pristine white laboratory coats over their dark denim jeans. Both scientists also sported brand new white sneakers and the professor wore his finest brown brogue shoes, which had been highly polished for the occasion.

Professor Brown felt incredibly proud. Both of his accomplishment and the fact that his daughter, Luna, had actually found the eggs and was now doing such a good job looking after the young dinosaurs. He was very glad that he had brought her to Walker County to work alongside him during the holidays.

The President welcomed them all with a broad, toothy smile. He shook Professor Brown's hand vigorously and complimented him on the discovery of the dinosaur eggs.

The President then turned his attention to the dinosaurs and remarked, "And it's a pleasure to meet you guys too. I've heard so much about you. I've heard that you can actually talk too. How about that?"

Oscar stepped forward, positioning himself in front of the other dinosaurs, and addressed the President in a clear and composed manner, "It is very nice to meet you Mr President, Sir, your Majesty of the world, Prince of the Stars and Stripes. We have watched you very much on the Tennyvision. We are impressed by what you have said about helping to stop climate change. Our ancestors were all killed by a similar problem millions of years ago. We want to help you stop climate change."

The President appeared utterly astonished, as did Luna and the Professor.

Oscar then walked toward the podium and mimicking the action of the Secret Service man who had tapped the microphone earlier,began to speak. "Testing, testing!"

He might not have received an official invitation to speak but speak he did. "Thank you, dear Mr President, your very Royal Majesty of the United Taters, people from the newspapers and the tennyvision. We are very pleased to be welcoming you here today."

Luna felt oddly proud. While Oscar's English was not yet perfect by any means, he remained intelligible and, up to this point, had avoided saying anything overly inappropriate. Well, aside from choosing to deliver a speech without actually being asked to do so.

Oscar continued to speak over the microphone, "We are the elected representatives of the dinosaurs found here in these caves after more than 66 million years by our very dear friend Luna. She has been teaching me English. But I am still learning – so be gentle with me."

"Our parents left us deep in the cave, gonzillions of years ago, because they knew they were gonna die due to a terrible problem with the sky or something and the weather, a bit like your climate change."

"We have come back to help you save you humans from yourselves. We want to make sure you don't become extincts...erm...extinct!" he corrected himself.

"It is gonna mean some changes though," he continued.

"You are going to need to find different ways to power every-fing. This oil and petrol stuff is no good for you! It is very bad for the environment."

"You need to take better care of the planet. You need to stop dumping lots of rubbish and plastic in the sea too," he continued emphatically. Astrid nodded in agreement with Oscar, her eyes carrying a serious expression.

"I mean come on dudes! You've messed up! Let's be honest! Let's get things cleaned up!" concluded Oscar.

The press and the camera crews were amazed, not only by the extraordinary sight of a talking dinosaur but also by the weight of Oscar's words.

Images of Oscar delivering his speech were broadcast worldwide, captivating people everywhere.

While absolute support and approval rippled through the crowd, the President was frowning. He hadn't expected this at all.

All he knew was that the biggest oil and gas companies, known as Big Oil, wouldn't be very happy at this development. He needed their financial donations to stay in power for another term. The presidential elections were coming very soon.

The President leaned in to whisper to one of his aides, "Perhaps, we should contact the Smithsonian National Zoo near the White House in Washington to see if they could accommodate three very friendly dinosaurs...indefinitely. Free board and lodgings! This would help keep them away from the media spotlight and I could also closely monitor their progress...and activities."

Unfortunately, or perhaps fortunately, depending on how you view it, Oscar caught wind of the President's whispered exchange with his aide. And with a distinct pop, all three dinosaurs vanished as swiftly as they had appeared earlier in the day.

Once again they were gone.

The media covered these events at length. For many months afterwards, long articles appeared in all major newspapers. TV channels carried non-stop discussions about the talking dinosaurs with an important message about protecting the planet and a taste for pizza and hip-hop music. But most dramatically, they reported how three large, talking dinosaurs had simply vanished before their very eyes with a loud pop.

Images of the three dinosaurs appeared in almost every publication you could imagine, from the Economist to Gardening World. Even Good Housekeeping magazine ran a piece discussing the advantages of foraging for unique pizza toppings in the wild. Dinosaur hunts were organised, offering handsome rewards for finding them.

Reports of sightings emerged from all corners of the globe - from Kathmandu to the Scottish Highlands. Despite these efforts, the dinosaurs were nowhere to be found.

They had become a media sensation overnight, only to completely disappear!

CHAPTER 7

The Dinosaurs' Return

L una lay in her bed, tossing and turning. She was back in Cambridge, England, tucked up in her cosy bedroom tucked beneath the stairs at her father's college. It had been more than two years since the dinosaurs had vanished, right under the noses of the President of the United States and his Secret Service agents.

Luna and Noah had continued to speak online most days. They had also met up a couple of times to go exploring caves together in both Argentina with their parents and in the United States, close to where Noah lived.

Luna was deeply distraught at what had happened. She missed all the dinosaurs terribly but she particularly longed for Oscar. She couldn't stop thinking about him. Luna wondered what he looked like now. He was already starting to become a very handsome dinosaur when she last saw him. She wondered if he could fly yet too, as he seemed to have feathers growing and wings forming. She also quietly giggled to herself about how Oscar had referred to the President of the United States as 'Him's Majesty' on live TV.

It was a few minutes past midnight and the sky was a deep, pitch black with only a faint glimmer of moonlight. The surroundings were calm and quiet. Luna could catch occasional sounds - a distant car engine, or the sporadic noise of students returning late, trying to convince the night porter at the college gates to let them in after curfew.

In Luna's room, the walls were plastered with posters of faraway lands with images of distant forests, canyons, rivers and oceans. An ancient, weathered wooden desk sat by the window, piled high with treasured books and magazines. The gentle hum of her 1930s desk lamp, a gift from her father, kept her company through the long hours of the night.

Outside, stone gargoyles perched along the edges of old buildings, their features frozen in silence – spitting and spewing out water whenever it rained. Cobblestone paths wound through courtyards where knowledge and learning echoed from every corner.

In the hush of the night, Luna found herself lost in her thoughts, her mind racing. Then, out of nowhere, she spotted what appeared to be two massive, radiant, orange eyes with a striking green outline, peering through her window. At first, she mistook them for the moon, except there were two of them and then they blinked at her.

She heard a faint whisper, "Yo Luna. It's me, it's your Oscar."

It was Oscar. And, boy, was he huge.

Her heart leapt! In an instant, she was out of bed and across the room, her feet barely touching the floor.

She swung the window open and hugged him tightly. Tears streamed down her cheeks, moistening his now fully grown, thick, pink plumage of feathers.

Stepping back, she gazed at him and noticed a splendid purple snout that had developed.

He had grown up to be a truly stunning, handsome and impressively large dinosaur. "Oscar! You look magnificent!" she exclaimed with joy, unable to contain her excitement.

"We've come to get you," said Oscar. "We are here to take you back with us. We are gonna save the world but we needs your help."

"We?" Luna stammered, her eyes darting around anxiously. And then, with a sudden double pop, both Alexander and Astrid appeared, equally huge and just as striking.

Astrid, the smallest of the three, was glistening. Her purple, green and blonde fish-like scales shining in the moonlight. Her eyes were mesmerising with a deep, captivating purple hue.

Alexander, the land dinosaur, was the largest among them. He was nearly the size of a small house, his now fully mature iridescent scales shimmering brightly in shades of red, orange, and turquoise. His deep green eyes held a steadfast gaze.

Luna marvelled at how well the dinosaurs had mastered the English language, despite the occasional small mistake or mispronunciation. It seemed that their unique approach to learning, through a shared consciousness, had truly paid off.

"We want you to help us run our new power company," said Oscar. "We are starting a social movement and a new kind of power company called 'Dino-Power' to help save the planet and you humans from extinction."

"And with our special technology you can still go on holiday and stay warm in the winter too...it's totally sick man!" exclaimed Astrid.

"Please say you'll join us, Luna? Please?" Alexander implored her. "We have set up all over the world, ready for you to be our leader."

"The humans will listen to another human and we trust you. We are all agreed. You are our choice," concluded Astrid emphatically.

Luna couldn't help but be filled with awe by their sheer intelligence and adaptability. It was evident that these creatures were far more than just mindless beasts; they were intelligent, thoughtful and capable of remarkable things.

Luna believed that they had the potential to achieve pretty much anything they set their minds to. How could she refuse such a wonderful invitation, Luna wondered. Her father, the Professor, had always encouraged her to follow her instincts and do what felt right - to "grab life by the horns", as he put it.

In less than a heartbeat, Luna grabbed her overnight bag and toothbrush, nodding in agreement. "Okay, I'm in," she confirmed.

"I think you might need your caving and climbing gear too," Oscar mumbled, his tone slightly embarrassed as he looked at his feet, avoiding direct eye contact with Luna.

Luna let out a resigned sigh. There was always something when it came to dealing with dinosaurs, she thought. She swiftly gathered her climbing boots, protective clothing and her helmet with a high-powered torch attached, tossing them all into a spacious canvas rucksack.

She was ready!

She clambered out of her window and grasped hold of Oscar. He extended a large wing to shield her, making sure both of them were completely invisible. Luna noticed a delightful smell, soon realising that it was Oscar's natural scent. It was gorgeous. If only you could bottle it, she thought!

She marvelled at how mature all the dinosaurs had become in their appearance. An overwhelming sense of happiness and pride filled her.

A policeman on a bicycle pedalled along the road at the street's end, prompting the other two dinosaurs to swiftly pop back into invisibility mode to avoid being noticed.

"Hold on to me," said Oscar. "We are going to fly. It will be a lot quicker. The others will follow on behind by land and river. They can catch us up."

With that announcement, Oscar soared into the sky, Luna gripping on tightly, as they began hurtling through the starry, pitch-black sky.

"Where are we going?" Luna inquired, feeling a touch of unease at the unknown.

"To our UK headquarters, dude. You'll see," Oscar responded in a calm and reassuring manner.

Luna held onto Oscar's thick neck feathers, burying her face in his plush plumage. It felt as cosy as a soft down pillow.

Luna felt the rush of wind through her hair as Oscar glided through the night sky, his mighty wings rhythmically flapping in powerful long thrusts. She was well-protected, surrounded by the warmth of his feathers.

As they flew, Luna gazed out at the twinkling stars above and the glowing lights of a city below. She marvelled at the beauty of the world and the abundance of incredible creatures that called it home.

"Oscar, do you ever get scared up here?" she asked, her voice barely audible over the rushing wind.

Oscar shook his head, his feathers rustling softly. "No, Luna," he said. "Flying is what I was born to do. It's in my blood, in my very soul. And when I'm up here, soaring through the sky, I feel truly alive."

Luna smiled, feeling a sense of peace settle over her. She knew that with Oscar by her side, she had nothing to fear.

Together, they continued to fly, their journey propelling them further and further towards their destination. And as Luna closed her eyes and drifted into sleep, she knew she was exactly where she was meant to be - with Oscar, her friend, the mighty and majestic dinosaur, on a magical journey through the night sky.

In what seemed like less than 20 minutes, they arrived at Ogof Ffynnon Ddu (or The Cave of the Black Spring, in plain English). Luna had heard of it from the caving and hiking magazines she and Noah liked to read, although she had never actually been there.

She had read somewhere that it was the UK's deepest cave complex, tucked away in a quiet corner of the Upper Swansea Valley in Wales. She also realised it would be an excellent hiding place, especially if you happened to be a massive, pink feathered, flying dinosaur.

Very few climbers had ever attempted to enter the cave and for very good reason, thought Luna. The main shaft alone is said to be three times the height of Big Ben. She had once asked Noah if he would like to try exploring it but she had received a decidedly lukewarm reaction from him to that suggestion. And he was one of the bravest cavers and climbers she had ever known. These dinosaurs were no fools when it came to hiding and they clearly knew their caves. Even her father had urged caution about exploring Ogof Ffynnon Ddu and he usually let Luna do anything she wanted.

Oscar flew directly into the spacious entrance and descended deep into the main shaft. He halted at a sizable ledge, positioned just before a stream coursing through the cave's lower reaches. Then, in front of her he tapped the rock face several times, following a curious and rhythmic sequence: "Click", "Click", "Tappety", "Tap", "Tip", "Tap", "Tip".

It reminded Luna of the tapping noise that came from inside the eggs when the dinosaurs had started to hatch back in the Appalachian Mountains. It was some sort of collective, secret Jurassic Morse code that only dinosaurs understood.

A large stone door slid smoothly open, revealing a vibrant scene inside. Hip hop music was playing loudly and hundreds of dinosaurs of various types, sizes and colours, were dancing together joyfully. Some were even wearing baseball caps, hoodies and sunglasses. Luna thought they all looked very cool. Cola was flowing, and pizzas seemed to be flying through the air in every direction

The party was held in Luna's honour. Her name adorned balloons and banners all around the large cave. Messages like 'Welcome Home Luna,' 'We Love you Luna,' and 'Luna for Prime Minister' were proudly displayed alongside numerous red heart decorations hung around the cave. Disco lights sent pulsating heart shapes into even the darkest corners of the cavern and Luna's name blinked on and off in an incredible light display.

The cave complex was a wondrous sight, transformed by the dinosaurs. Recycled and upcycled treasures adorned every corner. Colourful streamers made from repurposed materials hung from the stalactites, swaying gently as the dinosaurs danced. A large gleaming disco ball, created from fragments of old mirrors and shimmering baubles, scattered flashes of light across the makeshift dance floor.

The floor was a patchwork of salvaged tiles, painted blue, green, and purple. Large, brightly painted rocks served as makeshift benches for those who didn't want to strut their funky stuff. The dinosaurs had repurposed old wooden storage pallets and doors as tables. These were now piled high with an array of delicious pizzas. Upcycled lanterns cast a warm and inviting glow, guiding Luna through the cavern as she started to explore her new home.

"Wow! This place is amazing," said Luna taking it all in.

Luna's heart overflowed with emotion and tears of pure joy streamed down her cheeks. Before anyone could blink, she found herself dancing 'The Dinosaur'. Luna's movements embodied the playful spirit of a dinosaur, complete with spirited stomps, wild arm flails and twirls that imitated the joyful bounding of her prehistoric friends.

As she swayed and twirled, Luna couldn't help but notice the reaction of the actual dinosaurs around her. The sight of their human friend engaging in such a lively dance filled them with curiosity. Some tilted their heads in amusement while others tried to mimic Luna's exuberant moves in their own dinosaur way.

Oscar watched Luna with a gleam of amusement in his eyes. He let out a series of low, rumbling roars that echoed through the cave, as if applauding Luna's performance. Astrid, Hugo and Alexander joined in the fun by wiggling their tails and attempting to match Luna's crazy dance steps.

In one hand, Luna held a generous slice of the finest cheese and tomato pizza and in the other, a fizzy glass of sparkling cola. Although, she couldn't help but wonder if it truly was just plain cheese and tomato pizza - after all, you never quite know for sure with dinosaurs and their love for crazy toppings!

A familiar land dinosaur from her days in the Appalachian Mountains, named Tolstoy, extended both of his arms for a warm embrace. "We are so glad you have decided to join us on our mission, our dear friend Luna. We love you so much. We all missed you. You are the closest thing to a mother that we have. We will love and protect you always!" he said.

His skin, a dazzling blend of petrol blue, magenta and light turquoise, glistened in the disco lights. His turquoise eyes mirrored the sparkle of the glittering ball that twirled above Luna's head, suspended from the lofty cave ceiling.

Luna grinned, thinking about the fact that she had an enormous horde of large, magical dinosaurs always ready to guard and shield her from danger.

"Where are all the other dinosaurs?" Luna asked Tolstoy.

"When we realised the danger of us being taken prisoner to a zoo, or put into cages, we decided to disappear," Tolstoy replied.

"When the National Guard and Mr Professor, Sir, stopped searching for us, we split up and hid in the most remote caves all over the world."

"Oscar asked to come to the UK because of you, Luna. We are now in over 150 countries - all underground in caves. We've gone global," Tolstoy proclaimed proudly.

"Well, you certainly seem to have been very busy," agreed Luna.

Luna could see that this was no ordinary cave, not by a long shot. It had air conditioning, heating and an enormous multi-faceted pizza oven. There were also disco lights, a DJ podium with multiple decks and a hexagonal stage.

It was luxurious but displayed everywhere signs of the dinosaurs' commitment to protecting the planet, with an array of homemade and upcycled gadgets. Everything was made from reclaimed materials yet it had a certain technological sophistication that was utterly unique.

There were also all sorts of classic arcade games too, which were arranged along the cave's walls and desks crafted from repurposed doors - topped with reclaimed computers.

When Luna asked Oscar about this later, he explained that while they enjoyed living a fun life - when they weren't working to save the Earth - they wanted to do it in a way that would not cause problems for the environment or create unnecessary greenhouse gases. "It would be against our principles," Oscar told Luna firmly.

Oscar went on to tell Luna that they had built much more than what she could see here, and they were experimenting with all sorts of new ways to generate renewable energy and inventing new methods to clean up the environment.

"We are going to beat Big Oil," said Oscar with a mischievous twinkle in his eye. "We are already carbon neutral," he continued proudly.

He explained that they were already generating additional power, much more than they could possibly use, and were selling it to the National Grid. "But we need a bank account. I can't do it, I don't have a passport. And I can't write a signature," Oscar explained. "I don't have any thumbs so I can't hold a pen!"

Luna laughed at the idea of a huge pink dinosaur attempting to open a bank account - even if he did have a passport and thumbs. "Don't worry Oscar, I'll sort it out for you," Luna replied lovingly.

"Thanks Luna, I knew you would help us," said Oscar gratefully. "I'll show you more of our vinentions, I mean inventions, in the morning. They're totally dope."

Oscar also mentioned that he would give her the cheques they had received already from the National Grid so she could deposit them into a bank account on their behalf.

Oscar thought Luna should get some sleep now, although how on Earth one could ever sleep after the events of the night was completely beyond her.

On the way to showing Luna to her bedroom, Oscar did decide to tell her that Noah had just arrived at the new cave complex back in the Appalachian mountains where Luna and Noah had discovered them. He was going to help run things out in North America - if Luna agreed, that is.

Oscar suggested that Noah could be her 'number two'.

Luna told Oscar that this was fine. She liked Noah, had known him a long time and completely trusted him. He was also born in the 'United Taters', as Oscar kept calling the United States.

Oscar explained, "We found another completely undiscovered cave just a few miles from the cave where you discovered us, Luna. This new cave is very safe and we have created a headquarters for our North American operation," Oscar reported very seriously. He continued to explain that it was well hidden and had remained completely undetected by the authorities.

"We didn't dare go back to the old, original cave, where you found us," continued Oscar. "It would be far too dangerous," he concluded.

CHAPTER 8

The Start of a Beautiful Adventure

The next morning Luna woke up very early, full of anticipation and nervous energy. She paced around her cave bedroom, eager to get started. The wait for Oscar to come and get her seemed to go on forever.

Luna smiled as she looked around her new bedroom, taking in its unique and quirky design. It was unlike any other room she had ever seen with its modern yet rustic furnishings.

She gazed at her dressing table and couldn't help but admire the creativity and resourcefulness that had gone into crafting it. The legs were made from sturdy steel scaffolding which gave it an industrial, rugged appearance, while the repurposed wood top provided a sense of natural warmth and charm.

As she settled back into her spacious white canvas hammock waiting for Oscar to arrive, Luna felt a sense of comfort and peace wash over her. It was the perfect place to rest and relax and she was grateful for the serenity it offered.

Luna realised that in a world of chaos and confusion, it was often the simplest things that held true beauty - like the sun's warm glow, the gentle rustle of leaves, or the easy sway of a large canvas hammock in a Welsh cave full of hip hop and pizza crazy dinosaurs.

Luna knew that she was exactly where she was meant to be - in her own unique, quirky, and wonderful dino-world.

Resting on her hammock was an enormous pillow filled with fluffy feathers - pink feathers! At a glance she knew exactly where they had come from. She could see that the pillow had been crafted with great care and love. And upon the pillow was an embroidered red heart, exquisitely sewn, bearing her initials on it.

Luna could barely contain her excitement when she heard Oscar bounding down the corridor outside her room, humming a lively hip-hop tune to himself, stomping his feet and bashing the walls.

Oscar greeted her with a cool, "Yo dude!"

She ran towards him, as the dark rock door slid open, and hugged him tight, exclaiming "I can't wait to get started!"

"Breakfast first," Oscar said firmly. "There is a lot to do. You'll need your strength. Pizza OK with you?" he asked.

"Can I have a breakfast pizza with fried bacon and eggs, please? Maybe a few mushrooms too, but no funny dinosaur toppings please!" said Luna firmly.

Luna personally oversaw its creation in the expansive steam punk style kitchen located towards the rear of the cave, ensuring it met her exact instructions. The pizza had two large perfectly fried eggs, a generous serving of crispy streaky bacon, and a handful of sliced mushrooms for good measure.

She happily dug into her scrumptious breakfast pizza, relieved that it was free from any bizarre dinosaur toppings. No creepy crawlies, no strange spicy sauces, just the good stuff.

Oscar had suggested adding some chilli sauce or lemon curd to "liven it up" but Luna had responded with a very firm, "No!"

The kitchen boasted a massive, custom-built pizza oven that the dinosaurs themselves had created. It was constructed using tonnes of clay repurposed from the excavations that had been carried out since their arrival at the cave.

Now it was time for the much anticipated "World tour" as Oscar had described it. Which really meant he wanted to show her around 'his crib', as he kept referring to the cave.

Luna was eager to explore everything. The caves and corridors stretched out extensively, resembling a subterranean military compound. It was a unique blend of utilitarian grey passageways combined with enormous pizza ovens and reconditioned computer games. All of this was held together with miles and miles of tape and gallons of some special glue Oscar had made from tree sap.

First he took her down to the lower basement of this remarkable multi-level cave, dug deep into the Earth. The dinosaurs had excavated a lot of bedrock, clay, gravel and soil to house a massive homemade turbine. It was made from all sorts of recycled and upcycled plumbing equipment, pipes, and taps, including two old baths and a giant industrial fan.

As Luna and Oscar descended further into the lower basement, the air grew cooler and more damp. The walls of the cave were rough and uneven, glistening with moisture in some places. Dimly lit, homemade lanterns hung from hooks, casting a soft and flickering light that danced along the rocky surfaces. Water droplets dripped rhythmically from the ceiling, falling into small puddles on the ground.

They walked along a narrow pathway that wound through the cave, leading them deeper into the heart of the underground chamber. Stalactites and stalagmites jutted out from the ceiling, walls and floor - their jagged formations like frozen works of art. A small stream trickled by, its gentle babbling adding to the natural sounds echoing through the cavern.

Oscar explained that they had created a special "Geothermal Energy Heat Pump" as he called it. The dinosaurs had bored deep into the Earth and were now harvesting heat from the Earth's core, converting it into what Oscar referred to as "Dino Power".

"It generates enough power to house and feed over 300 dinosaurs - perhaps 500 at a push. It can also be used to cool down the cave in the summer," Oscar continued, seeming to have it all worked out.

"Damn clever, these dinosaurs!" thought Luna.

"We are now generating a lot more energy than we actually need so we are selling what we don't use to the National Grid. And it's all green energy," Oscar finally finished speaking and paused for breath.

It truly was an ingenious invention, Luna thought, wondering why humans hadn't figured out how to do something similar to help power everything. If a few ancient dinosaurs could work it out by surfing the internet, then why not humans? Maybe dinosaurs really were more advanced than humans.

They continued the tour around the cave and Oscar briefly showed her some of his other top secret inventions. There were three prototype vehicles designed to eliminate pollution and plastics from the air, oceans, and land.

The idea was that they would suck in large amounts of pollution and other waste and then convert it into low carbon energy.

"They beat, as they sweep, as they clean," announced Oscar proudly, fluffing out his chest.

"We can take you out for a spin in our vinentions very soon," Oscar said, obviously keen to move on with his whistle-stop world tour.

"I think you mean 'inventions'," Luna corrected Oscar for the umpteenth time, with a giggle.

After looking around the cave's many levels and bumping into a few of her old dinosaur friends, Luna said to Oscar, "Well, I'd better get to work then. I'll get everything set up for you, don't you worry!"

"We are going to give all our profits to charity to help save the Earth. All we need is some pizza base, some toppings, cola, some glue and tape to help us build our inventions. After that, we want to give it to charities that can help save the Earth, the humans and all the other creatures that live here."

"Okay, let's get cracking then," agreed Luna. "Where are all those bank cheques you told me about?"

Oscar motioned towards a large, heavy, dark, stone door, halfway down one of the corridors.

When he rolled back the door, it led to a big storeroom with an old, large wooden kitchen table that had almost certainly been reclaimed from a landfill site somewhere nearby.

Luna stood there in complete stunned silence. Before her lay an astonishing sight - a sea of cheques. There were hundreds, if not thousands, all payable to Dino Power Inc. They were strewn haphazardly on top of the sturdy, weathered table that occupied the centre of the room. The abundance of cheques had spilled over onto the floor, forming a scattered carpet that Luna had to wade through. It reminded her of piles of crisp leaves along a woodland walk in autumn. Except these crisp leaves were each worth tens of thousands of pounds each.

Luna noticed a small corner of the room where a small makeshift desk stood with a desktop computer sitting on it that she thought looked old school. Luna wondered to herself if this was Oscar's little hidey hole where he managed the financial side of Dino Power. Luna could imagine Oscar sitting there, his eyes twinkling with mischief as he counted and sorted the cheques and came up with new inventions.

"There are so many! I mean, how? But? Why? When?" blurted Luna, nearly lost for words.

She knelt down, her curiosity getting the better of her, and scooped up a handful of the cheques. As she glanced at them one by one, her eyes widened as she read the extraordinary amounts of money printed on each of them.

The first: £127,395.18 The second: £96,937.03. She couldn't believe her eyes.

"Wow!" she gasped. "These need to be paid into a bank quickly," Luna told Oscar.

Luna quickly settled herself at one of the many restored computers in the central recreation area of the cave. It was the same spot where the celebration in her honour had taken place the night before. She went online and ran a search on the internet for "How to start your own company". This was uncharted territory for her. After all, she was just a school kid.

But she soon discovered it was actually incredibly simple and before long, it was all done. Dino Power Inc. was up and running.

She wasn't sure if using the address "Care of Oscar (the Dinosaur), 1, Deep Cavern, The Cave, Ogof Ffynnon Ddu, Upper Swansea Valley, Wales" would really be suitable as the address for a multi-million dollar green energy company. So she checked the box for the fancy address in Berkeley Square, Mayfair, London W1J 6BD and paid a small additional fee to be able to use it as the company's official address.

Then Luna went ahead and opened an online bank account as well. For good measure, she also quickly designed a lovely logo online using an AI programme. The logo featured a picture of Oscar beside the words 'Dino Power' in a vibrant shade of green.

Lunu felt incredibly proud at what she had created in such a short time.

Oscar looked suitably impressed too. "Yes, you're slaying it, Luna! We could never have done this without you," he said in an adoring tone, now purring like he used to when he was young.

"Well, I simply followed the online instructions. It was much easier than I had expected," Luna said modestly. "As you say, it's all on the internet."

"Now, let's add up the total of all those cheques," she said to Oscar.

She grabbed a large old brown woollen blanket and tossed all the cheques into it. Carefully arranging it, she made sure to grasp each corner firmly and draw them together to prevent any cheques from slipping out. With this makeshift bundle in tow, she then hauled it from the storeroom across the stone corridor floor to her workspace by the computer.

As she did this, a couple of the cheques accidentally flipped out. She had to then backtrack and retrieve them individually.The sheer number of cheques made them surprisingly heavy when combined.

"Do you have something I can use to count them into?" she asked Oscar. "Maybe a large box? Or perhaps an old suitcase...or two?" she smiled at Oscar while she was speaking.

In the blink of an eye, Oscar leaped up and dashed into the cave next door, returning shortly with two large and slightly worn leather suitcases. "I found these at the nearby rubbish dump," he sheepishly confided in Luna.

This didn't faze Luna in the slightest. She shook her head gently, chuckling to herself as she did so.

It took her hours to add up the total value of all the cheques that Oscar had just tossed into the storeroom.

It didn't help that Oscar kept repeating everything Luna said as she calculated each sub-total, so she forgot where she had got to and had to start again. But after much checking, double-checking, and repeatedly telling Oscar to "Be quiet," Luna let out a deep sigh, followed by a long whistle.

And then, "330 million, 257 thousand, 767 pounds and 12 pence," she announced brightly, her smile broadening as she looked at Oscar. "Wow! Over £330 million!" she confirmed with excitement.

Luna was quite astonished by the surplus energy the dinosaurs had managed to generate and sell to the National Grid within such a brief time span.

No wonder Big Oil wasn't fond of any competition, or environmentally friendly alternatives to gas and oil, Luna thought to herself.

"And this was just in the UK. What on Earth will it all add up to if the other dinosaurs around the world have been doing as well as you guys?" asked Luna in a mildly alarmed voice.

Oscar smiled with pride. "We is going to be gonzillionnaires," he proclaimed, his excitement evident as his chest puffed up and his cheeks turned bright red.

"We certainly are, Oscar... We certainly are," Luna nodded in agreement.

Truth be told, Luna wasn't entirely sure how the staff at a small-town bank branch would react to a young girl showing up at their doors with two huge, worn suitcases filled with cheques totalling over £330 million.

Oscar agreed to fly her to the local bank branch the very next day, first thing in the morning.

Nervously, Luna asked him, "Oscar, you mentioned earlier that you have caves in 150 countries. Will you need me to set up bank accounts for all those countries too?"

"Er, yes," Oscar replied, his cheeks tinted with a blush. He looked at his feet, realising that Luna had spent the entire day sorting things out for just one country and there were still 149 more to go. The week ahead was going to be really long as Luna sorted everything out. It was vital to make sure that all the money was directly deposited into their bank account from now on. She had no plans of carrying suitcases filled with cheques around on a regular basis.

The next day, following another night of dancing to some incredible rap and hip-hop music and savouring a delicious vegetarian curry pizza, Luna was headed to the local bank branch in Swansea, where she had opened up the new bank account online.

She wrestled with the two massive bulging suitcases that Oscar had rescued from a local rubbish dump, ready to take them to the bank. The handles were fashioned from thick, double stitched leather, and the suitcases boasted large lockable brass clasps and straps that wrapped around them, which was fortunate since there was no key to lock the cases with.

Luna embarked on her journey in first-class comfort, aboard her very own private pink dinosaur jet (referred to as 'Oscar Air' by Oscar). They sped through the early morning sky, deftly avoiding two small planes and a helicopter along the way. As they whooshed over a field, they startled a small group of sheep and sent them running from one side of their field to the other.

She pushed her head out a few inches from out under Oscar's wing as they flew and watched as rows of hedges and trees tore past on either side of them. Oscar's wings flapped long and hard propelling them forward faster than a military fighter plane. And even then, suddenly, Oscar seemed to up his speed and propelled them even faster, so that the countryside was a complete blur and Luna's eyes watered.

Then there came a loud 'crack' in the air. It was so loud it startled Luna!

"We have just gone supersonic" Oscar announced, his voice piercing through the rushing wind. Luna swiftly decided to duck her head back down behind one of Oscar's robust pink wings for safety.

The two worn leather suitcases were filled to the brim with hundreds and hundreds of crumpled cheques. They were so stuffed that Luna had to grip the leather handles very tightly to prevent them from slipping out of her grasp, as they raced through the air.

Oscar touched down with a thump in an empty supermarket parking lot, near the bank. Since it was early, there weren't many people around just yet. So nobody saw them land.

Luna lugged the bulging suitcases toward the small bank branch situated within Swansea's Indoor Market. Her wrists were beginning to ache.

Luna viewed everyone who approached her on the street with suspicion. She was worried that someone might try to rob her if they knew what the cases held. However, she quickly comforted herself, thinking that it was highly unlikely anyone could know that she was transporting over £330 million in her pair of weathered leather suitcases.

That said, she couldn't help but find a man across the road highly suspicious. He had mean, spiteful eyes that were far too close together and a sharp, thin face that reminded Luna of a hatchet. As she continued to drag the two old suitcases up the street, she felt he was following her and this thought lingered in her mind.

She stopped every so often to catch her breath and make sure that nobody was following her. After a while, she didn't see the hatchet-faced man again, which left Luna feeling very relieved.

Finally, she reached the small bank branch, feeling hot and flustered. At first glance, the bank clerk seemed somewhat doubtful about a young girl like Luna arriving with millions of pounds' worth of cheques. But, after a moment's hesitation, she swiftly escorted Luna into a small back office and completed all the necessary paperwork for her.

"Will you be making regular deposits like this?" inquired the young bank clerk, a slightly concerned look in her eyes.

"No, I believe future payments will most likely come through direct transfers from now on," Luna responded, her tone making it sound as if it were a routine matter for her to drop off over £330 million in crumpled checks at her local bank branch.

She strolled back to the supermarket car park where she had left an invisible Oscar leaning against the dumpster. No doubt he had been rummaging through it to find things he could salvage and repurpose.

However, upon her return he was nowhere to be seen and the car park had become a lot busier. Yet, Luna didn't have to wait for too long before he made his presence known to her.

"Yo, I am here!" she heard Oscar whisper in her ear.

Then, she sensed an invisible wing grasp her as Oscar pulled her up onto his back - sheltering her beneath his wing.

Now both invisible, they soared off toward the cave, hidden from an unsuspecting world.

Upon their return to the cave, Oscar beamed with pride as he showed Luna a collection of copper piping and brass taps he had rescued from the dumpster in the supermarket car park. "This will be the perfect thing for the new water filterafication system I've got planned for the cave," he informed Luna. He was visibly excited.

Luna laughed at his mispronunciation of 'filtration'. She guessed it was a difficult word for a young dinosaur and politely decided not to mention it.

Luna smiled. "Oscar, you never cease to invent new things and come up with incredible ideas, do you?" she told him, giving his neck a gentle hug and a kiss.

Oscar beamed. He wanted nothing more than for Luna to appreciate the efforts he and the other dinosaurs were making.

"Why buy what you can make? That is my motto," declared Oscar modestly.

"Well, I think you are doing a lot more than just making these amazing inventions," Luna replied. "You are going to change the way we all live!" Oscar grinned a broad smile and blushed brightly at this.

CHAPTER 9

All Aboard Oscar's Eco-airship

A week later, with all the hard work now done, everything was finally set up and it was time for an adventure.

Oscar had promised Luna a reward for all her help in getting everything organised with the bank accounts. He had agreed that she could accompany him and some of their other dinosaur friends to test drive the different prototype vehicles they had designed and built. Luna would be able to personally witness how these vehicles removed pollution from the atmosphere and converted it into pure, natural Dino Power.

In total Luna had paid over $28 Billion into the various company bank accounts of Dino Power Inc all over the world. And Oscar had insisted that Luna immediately donate $5 billion to some of his favourite charities around the world that helped to protect wildlife, clean up the seas and oceans and work to stop the rainforests from being cut down.

Dino Power was already starting to make a difference.

"Hey Luna, it is time for your test drive in my eco-airship. You are gonna love how it works, fam! It can hit Mach 2 but uses only natural, clean Dino Power. No creating air pollution with these dope rides!" explained Oscar.

Luna rolled her eyes at Oscar's attempts to speak the street slang he had heard on the hip hop records he loved so much. But she decided not to try correcting him. She thought you shouldn't judge people because of the way they speak, only by their actions.

"I can't wait!" answered Luna. "I'm sooo excited!"

Luna could hardly contain herself as she stepped onto the deck of Oscar's hand-built eco-airship. It was a one-of-a-kind DIY engineering marvel that challenged both logic and convention.

The airship was fashioned from a repurposed old bathtub, reclaimed pipes, and taps, and featured a giant fan at the back. What's more, it was all held together by lots of tape and buckets full of Oscar's special homemade glue.

The airship's fan engine roared into life and Luna felt the deck beneath her vibrating as they soared into the sky. As they raced higher and higher, Luna gazed in wonder as the world below gradually shrank beneath them.

People turned into tiny dots on the landscape, cars looked like bright metallic beetles slowly moving along busy roads, and lakes seemed to be just ponds with small white dots, which Luna could see were people on small boats if she strained her eyes.

But it wasn't just the airship itself that was remarkable. Oscar had also created a revolutionary new engine that turned air pollution into clean energy. The airship was powered as it flew - by its own Dino Power, a carbon-free source of energy that Oscar said would help to save the planet. And then, the airship simply plugged in overnight after a hard day's work to save any remaining energy that hadn't been used during the flight. It actually created spare energy, rather than using any up.

The view was breathtaking as they flew, and she felt a sense of awe at the world's beauty beneath her. She understood that Oscar's inventions would make a real difference in the world once they were in full production. They would play a vital role in fighting pollution and addressing climate change, while also meeting the need for heating, lighting, and powering everything that mankind needed.

Not to mention, Oscar's airship was great fun and super-fast! Oscar was humming a tune to himself as they flew.

"How do you come up with all these amazing ideas, Oscar?" Luna asked inquisitively, interrupting his humming.

"I don't really know Luna. I just learnt everything on the internet and then it was just really obvious to me!" Oscar answered in a very matter of fact voice. "It's all things governments and big business already know," he concluded.

"Then why don't they do what you are doing?" Luna inquired.

"I don't know why these business dudes just ignore what is staring them in their face? It seems crazy," Oscar replied. "Maybe it is to do with making money?" he suggested.

"Hmm..." Luna said with a quizzical expression on her face."

"Yeah, that could be it!" Oscar responded. "Yeah, I think that is probably the reason," he concluded.

"But they are always saying how much they want to become carbon neutral," Luna added.

"Politicians don't always tell the truth, Luna," Oscar murmured, a slightly enigmatic expression on his face and a knowing glint in his eye. "Nor do big businesses. They are only really interested in themselves."

He quickly brushed aside these dark thoughts about dishonest politicians and the powerful people from Big Oil, who say one thing yet do quite the opposite. He wanted to enjoy the day with Luna.

As they soared through the air, Luna could see the airship's filters in action, capturing pollution and transforming it into rich, green energy. She felt a rush of excitement, realising that she was a part of something really important.

"This is dope, dude!" said Luna, attempting to speak street lingo like Oscar and the other dinosaurs.

Oscar smiled and changed the subject. "I heard that Noah is doing a great job out in the United Taters. He is slaying this business stuff." Oscar reported matter-of-factly. "He's been helping in Mexico, Brazil and Canada too. We've got caves everywhere you know."

"I'd love to go see Noah one day soon," replied Luna. She missed his friendship and sense of humour. She pictured his dark almond-shaped eyes and short coiled hair, and a mile of white, beautiful smile spread across her face.

Inspired by this conversation, she decided to video call Noah as soon as she got back to the cave. The last week or so had just been too busy to do anything other than get Dino Power Inc up and running, but she promised herself to call Noah tonight.

"I'll take you to see Noah and his cave headquarters soon, dude," promised Oscar, realising that Luna was missing Noah badly.

Eventually, as they started to descend, the view of the world below grew larger once more. Luna looked down at a picturesque stone village nestled among rolling hills. The village had cobblestones in the streets, charming cottages, and an ancient church with a tall spire.

"Wow, look at that village," Luna exclaimed.

It was a beautiful day but Luna could see that there was some flooding in the valley below from a recent storm.

Then she noticed a young couple outside the church, dressed in elegant wedding attire. A wedding photographer scurried around in a frenzy of activity, capturing candid shots of the couple, their families, and friends. The guests were trying to avoid puddles and the muddy grass verges caused by the recent rain.

"Oh look! A wedding," Luna cried out with excitement.

"That photographer is more energetic than a squirrel on caffeine," joked Oscar, smiling as he flapped his wings slowly.

An old Rolls Royce was parked outside the church graveyard, bedecked with ribbons and flowers. Clearly, it was waiting for the happy couple, ready for their getaway once the photographer had finished taking all the pictures of their very special day. It was a beautiful countryside scene that was likely being repeated all over the world every week by thousands of people.

"It's so beautiful," Luna exclaimed, her face a blend of awe and sheer joy.

Oscar smiled. He loved seeing Luna this happy.

Upon landing on a small hill in the countryside, Luna felt so at ease with the world, and she relaxed. Stepping off the airship, she felt as if she had just experienced something truly magical.

Oscar had thoughtfully brought a picnic with him - consisting mostly of pizza, of course!

As they sat in the warm sun on a cosy red and blue checked woollen blanket, hungrily munching on their pizzas and chatting about the latest computer games, Luna spotted a troop of large orange ants marching determinedly across the hilltop. They appeared a bit bedraggled and fatigued from the heat.

"Hey, Oscar, look over there. Those ants seem to be on some kind of mission. They almost look like they're in the army or something," Luna exclaimed, pointing at the ants.

"Oh, those guys? Perhaps they're milit-ANTs," quipped Oscar, smiling and raising his eyebrows nervously, not sure how his silly joke had landed.

Luna giggled at Oscar's playful comment.

"Jokes," Oscar concluded sheepishly.

"Yeah, obvs!" came Luna's response immediately. "You and your 'jokes' Oscar."

The ants were very friendly and spoke to Luna and Oscar.

Their leader explained what they were doing. "Hello there! We've had to move uphill out of the valley to avoid the flooding," he explained. "Now we're experiencing a bit of a heatwave, you see. The weather keeps changing so frequently. We just can't keep up with it."

It was scorching, and the ants were getting fried by the sun.

Luna's face showed genuine concern for the tiny creatures facing the challenges of their changing environment.

"A heatwave? That must be tough on all of you," exclaimed Luna.

The ant leader nodded, delighted that someone was actually listening to their plight. "It is. Our ant hill is getting too warm, and the journey to find food is becoming more and more treacherous," he told Oscar and Luna.

"That's tough, little buddies. Is there anything we can do to help?" Oscar said to the ants, sympathetically.

"Thank you for asking. If you find any shade or a cool spot, that would be a great help. Also, if you have any spare water or food, that's like nectar to us," answered the leader of the ants.

"It's not easy when everything around you keeps changing, huh?" asked Luna.

"Indeed. But we're ants. We adapt. We persist," the ant leader answered in a stoic tone.

Oscar then handed the ants a huge slice of his pizza to help them through the day and provide them with the energy needed to finish their long, steep march up the hill.

Luna found this a comical sight, considering how tiny the ants were and how massive the slice of pizza was!

The ants, however, were very grateful and eagerly accepted Oscar's offering. Struggling to lift and carry it, taking turns, the ants could only just carry the pizza slice.

Luna grinned and told the ants, "Enjoy the pizza, little friends! It's our way of saying, keep up the good work."

Oscar chuckled and made an additional gesture, "If you're looking for some shade, check out this origami sunshade I just made for you from a discarded piece of thin card."

Oscar offered the origami sunshade to the ants, who appeared both entertained and impressed by his creativity.

The ants then scurried away military style, skilfully balancing the huge slice of pizza and the delicate sunshade with remarkable coordination.

As the ants continued on their mission, Luna and Oscar exchanged glances, a shared understanding of the challenges faced by even the tiniest members of the earth's population.

Luna and Oscar watched as they rotated positions within the group, sharing both the load and the shade as they went.

"Look at them, Oscar," Luna said, "Such incredible teamwork!"

Oscar nodded; the admiration was evident in his eyes. "Nature has its own ways of showing us how to work together," agreed Oscar.

As the ants vanished over the hill, Luna's expression turned sombre.

"It's a reminder that we need to take better care of our world," said Luna. As she watched them fade into the distance, she felt a pang of sadness and guilt - it wasn't fair that these tiny creatures had to suffer due to the actions of humans. "If this is happening on this hill, it must be happening on millions of other hills all around the world," said Luna.

"Oscar, what can we do to help?" Luna inquired, turning to her dinosaur friend.

Oscar thought for a moment, his large eyes scanning the landscape. "Well, people could start by reducing their own carbon footsteps...I mean footprints," he said, correcting himself. "They could walk, or ride bikes, instead of driving cars, use less energy at home, and stop using plastic. All these things can help reduce the impact of you humans on the planet," he added, looking wiser than his years.

Luna nodded, determined to do her part. "And what about your new inventions?" she asked. "Can they help too?"

Oscar smiled. "Absolutely," he declared emphatically. "My carbon-free power inventions are still in their development stage, but once they're ready, Luna, they'll be a game-changer. The whole world will be able to generate clean energy without releasing harmful greenhouse gases into the atmosphere."

Luna's face lit up with a bright grin, her eyes shining with hope. "That's amazing, Oscar," she said. "I know we can't solve all the problems on our own, but every little bit helps. And who knows, maybe one day those ants will be able to come back down the hill and live in a world that's a little cooler and a little kinder."

Oscar nodded, flexing his beautiful pink feathers in agreement. "We'll do our best, my dear Luna," he said. "One slice of pizza at a time," he joked. He then devoured the last piece of his pizza, this time topped with beef slices, stewed prunes and pink custard.

This was one pizza that Luna didn't plan on sharing any time soon. She found the combination rather revolting if she were honest.

She chuckled, remarking, "I really don't know how you eat some of these toppings on your pizzas." Oscar just grinned and kept quiet, happily chomping away at the pizza, prune juice dripping everywhere, with a huge smile on his face.

The airship zipped back to the cave at a remarkable speed. Flocks of birds, mainly swifts, joined Luna and Oscar on their return journey, accompanying them along the way. The birds darted and soared in unison, as they all flew along together. Hugo and Orinoco also joined them in the air for the last stretch of their journey, twisting and turning together in the powerful winds along the Welsh coast.

On a nearby cliff, Luna could see a man with a giant pair of binoculars looking out to sea. She thought for a moment he looked a lot like the hatchet-faced man she had seen in Swansea, the day she paid in all the cheques at the local bank branch. It couldn't be. Surely not, she thought. She decided it was probably just her imagination working overtime, and that she was mistaken.

Luna and Oscar arrived back at their cave, just as the sun was starting to fade. It had been a tiring yet very enjoyable day.

Luna scrambled off Oscar's airship, stretched her limbs and let out an enormous yawn, the exhaustion from the day's adventure settling in. The long flight back had been both thrilling but tiring, and she was relieved to return to the safety and comfort of her cave home nestled high in the Welsh hills.

As they made their way into the cave, Luna couldn't help but feel a sense of awe and wonder at the natural beauty that surrounded her. The cool rock walls were decorated with shimmering crystals and colourful stalactites, and the tunnel was bathed in the warm glow of bioluminescent plants.

Before bed Luna remembered to call Noah. She enjoyed chatting to him via a video link. His cave looked a bit more corporate than the one in Wales, with sheets of brushed steel lining the cave walls, apparently reclaimed from an old office block that was being demolished in Denver.

Luna and Noah ended talking for over an hour about the Dino Powered social movement they were now helping to drive.

"Can you believe how quickly it's catching on?" Luna remarked, her eyes gleaming with excitement.

"Yeah, it's incredible," Noah replied, adjusting his glasses. "People from all around the world are getting involved. The impact is way beyond what we ever imagined."

Luna nodded, a smile playing on her lips. "And the best part is that it's not just about clean energy. It's a mindset, a social movement working towards a more sustainable and harmonious way of living."

Noah leaned closer to the screen. "You're right, Luna. It's about showing the world that we can make better choices for the planet and still live fulfilling lives. It's about proving that we don't have to sacrifice our comfort for the well-being of the Earth."

Luna chuckled, "Exactly! And we're just getting started. I can't wait to see what we can achieve together."

Before she knew it was now getting late, so she said to Noah, "Hey, it's getting late here, I better go. I'll come and visit you very soon. Oscar says he'll fly me over to see you."

By then, it was definitely bedtime. With another exciting adventure on the horizon tomorrow, this time with Astrid, Luna knew she would need every bit of energy she could muster to make the most of it.

CHAPTER 10

Out on the Open
Sea with Astrid

The next day, Luna had arranged to join Astrid, the magnificent sea dinosaur, for an outing to test the sea vehicle that Oscar had designed. Oscar had dubbed it the 'Sea Trials', and it was time to see what the vehicle could do on the open ocean.

Astrid's boat, if you could even call it a boat, was tucked away in a small cave nearby, along the Welsh coastline in Pembrokeshire. Oscar flew them there in his airship.

The watercraft looked like a mix between a boat and a very wide submarine, featuring a spacious front cockpit with a retractable glass dome that seemed perfect for underwater exploration.

Painted on its side was 'DINO 2', and it had large mechanical claws for grabbing plastic waste, ropes, and abandoned fishing nets from the ocean.

The entire construction seemed to be pieced together from reused parts of old boats and perhaps even sections of an old hovercraft.

Soon, Luna and Astrid found themselves inside the craft. With Astrid piloting it, they smoothly guided the sea vehicle out of the cave, emerging into the bright sunlight.

Luna and Astrid settled into the roomy cockpit, Luna's eyes growing wide as she took in the amazing view stretching out before them.

"This glass dome is incredible! The visibility is unreal. I can see for miles," Luna exclaimed, her voice tinged with awe.

Gazing at the rocky coastline while heading north, Luna couldn't help but express her admiration for the breathtaking beauty of the Welsh coast.

"The Welsh coast is truly something else!" Luna marvelled.

As DINO 2 smoothly glided into the open ocean, Luna's heart raced, captivated by the vastness of the water surrounding them.

"The ocean holds so many secrets, Luna. We are only just scratching the surface," Astrid remarked wistfully.

Journeying steadily north toward the Orkney Isles, just off the Scottish coast, Luna found herself enchanted by the lush green hills meeting the expansive blue sea.

"Look at those waves crashing against the rocks," Luna said, her enthusiasm beaming. Astrid smiled, thoroughly enjoying Luna's infectious love for the sea.

"It is nature's artwork, Luna. Each wave is a masterpiece," Astrid replied.

Amid the rhythmic sounds of the ocean, Astrid turned to Luna with curiosity. "So, Luna, tell me more about your life in Cambridge. What's it like living at a university?"

"Oh you know, it's like anywhere I guess, in the end you just take it for granted."

"I actually really like Cambridge though. It is like a small market town with lots of very old historic buildings, even though it is a city."

"It's got a nice river that runs right through it too, although I think it might not be deep enough for your antics, Astrid," said Luna.

Astrid laughed. "I saw the river when I came to collect you that night with Oscar. It looked lovely but Oscar wouldn't let me swim in it in case I drew too much attention to myself."

"Yes, I think you might have caused a bit of a stir if you had done that," agreed Luna.

As Luna marvelled at the incredible technology at work, Astrid turned to her with a broad dino grin. "We dinosaurs might have been extinctified for gonzillions of years, but we have a few tricks up our sleeves," she said, her eyes twinkling with amusement. "Oscar is very clever, you know."

Luna nodded, her mouth agape, simply taking it all in. Riding on this amazing watercraft with a sea dinosaur was already a huge adventure, but what really caught her imagination was how it was helping the environment.

As they carefully picked up tonnes of plastic, ropes, and old fishing nets from the water, Luna's curiosity grew even stronger. She wanted to learn more about this incredible process and how it could make a difference to the world.

"Astrid, this is amazing!" Luna exclaimed, adding, "How do you even turn plastic into power?"

Astrid smiled warmly, eager to explain the technology in a way that left Luna feeling amazed and wanting to learn more. "It's all about harnessing the energy that's stored in the bonds of the plastic molecules," she explained.

"We use a process called pyrolysis to break down the plastic into smaller molecules, which can then be used to generate energy. And the best part is that the process is completely carbon-free - so we are not only removing plastics from the oceans, we are also producing clean energy with it too," concluded Astrid. "It is win, win!"

Luna gasped, "That's incredible! I had no idea that was even possible."

Astrid smiled warmly, adding, "There's always more to learn. You can never know everything. And with your help, Luna, maybe we can spread the word and inspire others to take action against pollution of the oceans."

Luna nodded, feeling inspired and grateful for this amazing experience.

Luna's attention was suddenly drawn to a pod of playful dolphins leaping in and out of the water. Their energy was infectious and Luna couldn't help but smile as she watched their crazy antics.

"Dolphins! They're so joyful," Luna exclaimed, raising her voice to be heard over the roar of the sea.

"They remind us to enjoy every moment, Luna," responded Astrid, her eyes reflecting wisdom beyond her years.

As the dolphins continued their aquatic ballet, Astrid continued, "You know, Luna, the oceans are home to an incredible array of creatures, big and small.

From the majestic whales to the tiniest plankton, each one plays a crucial role in maintaining the balance of marine life. It's like a grand symphony and every participant has its own unique melody."

Luna listened intently, captivated by Astrid's words.

"We must protect them all, Luna, just like we protect our friends in the cave. The oceans are vast and mysterious, but they're also fragile. Human actions, like polluting our seas and overfishing, threaten them. It's our responsibility to ensure that the wonders beneath the waves continue to thrive for generations to come," Astrid declared with conviction.

Before long, DINO 2 approached the picturesque Orkney Isles, a cluster of islands off the Scottish coast. Luna took in the stunning landscape – made up of rolling green hills, quaint villages, and historic stone structures. The view must resemble the time when dinosaurs last roamed the Earth, thought Luna.

"It's like a hidden paradise," Luna muttered under her breath, unable to believe her eyes.

"Nature's wonders are scattered everywhere, just waiting to be explored," Astrid replied with a gentle nod.

After a while, they reached a tiny, uninhabited powder-white sandy island.

In the shallow waters around the island, Luna spotted a multitude of crabs and shrimps. She noticed one family of shrimps proudly wearing aluminium ring pulls from cans of fizzy drinks as earrings. While they looked rather fancy, Luna couldn't help but feel a bit sad that such rubbish had ended up in the sea and the food chain in the first place.

She pointed this out to Astrid, who shrugged and said, "It just has to stop, my dear Luna, so many sea creatures are being killed or maimed every year by all the rubbish and plastic that is in the oceans and rivers!"

Soon, a beautiful, large, green sea turtle swam alongside Astrid and Luna. The sea turtle said to them, "My necklace is getting very tight for me. Could you help at all, it's starting to hurt?" He spoke with a high, gurgling, ethereal voice that had a sing-song quality to it.

Luna saw to her dismay that the turtle had a very tight rope, tied to a faded orange water buoy, wrapped around his neck. It was cutting deep into his flesh, slowly strangling him. Luna signalled the turtle to come a little closer and Astrid carefully snipped the tight rope with her razor-sharp claws.

The turtle gulped and rubbed his neck in relief, grateful that he was no longer being strangled by the discarded rope.

"Thank you so much," the turtle gurgled thankfully. "I was starting to worry. I couldn't hunt for food anymore."

As the turtle swam away singing an ancient song of the seas, Luna felt a mix of emotions. She was relieved that they had been able to help the turtle, but also angry that humans had created this problem in the first place.

"We have to take action," Luna declared, her voice brimming with a mix of anger and resolve. "We can't simply stand by and watch our oceans and waterways being harmed by this kind of reckless behaviour."

Astrid nodded, her large eyes reflecting the same determination. "You're right, Luna," she said.

As they continued to explore the small island, Luna and Astrid worked together to collect as much trash, plastic, and litter as they could. They filled up a total of 24 giant sacks with the debris they had gathered from the island.

As they sailed away from the island, Luna knew that this was just the beginning of their efforts. There was still a lot of work to be done, but with her dino friends by her side, she was ready to face the challenge.

With their work for the day complete, they turned back towards the Welsh coast as the sun began to set. As they sailed homeward, Luna watched the waste they had collected turn into green energy, thanks to Astrid's savvy craft.

Again, high on a cliff near their cave, Luna saw the distinct outline of a man with large binoculars. This time he was clearly watching Astrid and Luna sailing along the coastline in DINO 2. She started to quietly worry about who the hatchet-faced man was and why he was watching her.

Despite her anxiety, Luna was again ready to hit her bed that night after an exhausting day.

The next day, Luna was due to meet with Alexander for her third and final adventure, test driving Oscar's amazing eco-friendly land vehicles. It was designed to clean up pollution on the ground, while generating more Dino Power than it consumed.

Though Luna wasn't entirely sure how it worked, she trusted that Alexander would explain it all to her.

As she climbed into her hammock, she caught a faint whiff of Oscar's distinct and gorgeous scent, probably lingering in the pink feathers he had used to stuff her pillow. "I wonder what adventures tomorrow holds," she thought to herself, as she quickly drifted off into a sleep in her cosy hammock.

Alexander Wows The Crowds at The Village Fair

The next morning, Luna woke up early and quickly dug into her favourite breakfast pizza, topped with two fried eggs, crispy bacon, mushrooms, and a big dollop of tomato ketchup. "Yummy!" Luna exclaimed.

Alexander joined her, munching on a huge pizza of his own, topped with gorgonzola cheese, a sprinkle of large iridescent beetles, and a few raw anchovies. He wrinkled his nose up in mild disgust at the tomato ketchup that Luna was dipping her pizza in, reaching instead for a big spoonful of peanut butter and spreading it thickly across his pizza.

"Each to their own," thought Luna.

With an affectionate wave from Oscar and Hugo, they set off on foot from the dirt track that led to an area of shingle close to the entrance of the cave. Alexander had hidden his vehicle between two huge rocks, tucked out of sight under a layer of camouflage netting and branches. Oscar had found the netting at an abandoned army base near Salisbury on one of his late night stealth flights.

Before long, they found themselves cruising down the road at speed. The vehicle worked without any obvious power source, gliding swiftly along the winding country lanes.

As Alexander and Luna cruised along, the vehicle hummed softly, its rhythmic vibrations. Luna couldn't help but be struck by the ingenuity of the hand-built technology surrounding her. The eco-vehicle was a testament to the dinosaurs' creativity, collecting pollution and transforming it into clean, sustainable energy.

Lost in her thoughts, Luna reflected on the series of adventures she had experienced throughout the week. These innovative vehicles, including the one she was in now, represented a beacon of hope amid the environmental challenges humanity faced. They were more than just modes of transportation; they were symbols of change, ingenuity, and the urgent need for sustainable solutions.

Gazing out of the vehicle's window, Luna's thoughts took a sombre turn. The beauty of the countryside they were travelling through couldn't completely dispel the underlying sadness she felt. She thought about the impact of human actions on the planet, the devastation left in the wake of careless exploitation and human greed for profit. She whispered to herself, "Humans have wrecked so much of this planet."

Alexander, ever perceptive, sensed Luna's shift in mood. "Luna," he said in his comforting rumble. "Remember, we're here to make things right. Every step we take with these vehicles, every innovation we introduce, is a step toward healing the Earth. It's not just about the machines, it's about inspiring change. We are pioneers in a journey to restore balance, and you're a crucial part of it."

Luna managed to break a small smile, appreciating Alexander's attempt to lift her spirits. "You're right, Alexander. We are making a difference, aren't we?"

"Absolutely," affirmed Alexander. "And don't forget, we're only just getting started."

Luna and Alexander arrived at a beautiful village green, deep in the English countryside. The air was filled with the joyful melodies of singing birds, perched high up in the immaculately manicured lime trees that bordered the road. Luna's eyes widened in awe as she took in the serene beauty of the scene before her.

The village green looked like a bright emerald handkerchief, framed by worn, ancient flagstone paving slabs and surrounded by charming medieval stone houses.

"Wow, this village looks straight out of a fairy tale!" exclaimed Luna.

"Does that make me the dashing knight who brought you here?" teased Alexander, smiling.

Luna playfully rolled her eyes and stepped out of the vehicle.

"If it does, that must make me a fairytale princess," she replied.

They shared a playful laugh, as they began walking towards the village green. Alexander was pleased that Luna seemed to have cheered up a bit.

On the village green a country fair was in full swing, and it seemed like the entire village had turned out to enjoy the festivities. Little old ladies in hand-knitted cardigans were selling jams and chutneys in glass jars to the villagers. Others were judging vegetables of every size and shape.

Music played loudly and colourful bunting adorned the trees surrounding the green.

Luna laughed, shaking her head. "Who would've thought we'd end up at a country fair today?"

As Luna and Alexander arrived, the lively music came to an awkward stop, and the vibrant colours of the fair seemed to lose their brilliance. In some respects this was hardly surprising. After all, it's not every day that a giant dinosaur, travelling by a hand-built, steel, eco-vehicle with a grabbing claw on the front, arrives at a country fair. The initial reaction from the villagers wasn't one of awe but of absolute terror.

Gasps rippled through the crowd. Some froze, rooted to the spot, while others took a few steps back, eyes wide with fear. The festivities transformed in a matter of seconds into a moment of collective panic.

Fortunately, before mass hysteria could completely get the better of the villagers, a young boy stepped forward. His eyes sparkled with excitement as he assured the others that he had seen these dinosaurs on television.

The boy told the crowd that these dinosaurs were friendly and harmless, emphasising that the President of the United States himself had even met them, and they hadn't eaten him. Slowly, the tension lifted, replaced by curiosity and amazement at the unexpected spectacle unfolding before them.

Soon everyone was hugging Alexander and taking selfies with him on their mobile phones. Before long, Alexander's presence at the tiny village fair had gone viral on the internet. Hundreds of people started arriving in cars to see this amazing dinosaur and his funky land craft.

Luna quickly suggested to Alexander that it might be better to keep a lower profile, although it was no easy feat when you were almost as big as one of the large trees that bordered the village green.

Alexander turned himself invisible with a pop, leaving Luna to explain the sudden disappearance of her large dinosaur friend to the growing crowd of increasingly over-excited people.

"Yeah, sorry, he often just pops off like that," Luna explained.

Two of the old ladies selling jams and chutneys soon came to her rescue and whisked her off to the village hall, where a few of their friends were knitting some brightly coloured pullovers out of old wool. They explained to Luna that they were all members of the local Village Committee and made all of their own food and clothing out of recycled materials and fruit picked from their gardens and the woodland and lanes around the village.

Alexander soon reappeared with a resounding pop, half scaring the little old ladies to death, before charming them with his endearing and friendly manner. He had to stoop down low to fit inside of the cramped village hall.

He clearly liked what he had heard about how these old ladies were making everything from repurposed materials, or fruit and vegetables that would have just been wasted.

This very much played to the whole approach of Alexander, Astrid, Oscar and the other dinosaurs, particularly as they were using old wool that was being recycled from previous garments into new items of clothing. He told them that he was very proud of them for reusing old wool to make new clothes.

"I can help you, if you like, by building you a knitting machine that will help you to knit hoodies, more quickly," said Alexander obligingly.

"We don't wear hoodies," said one of the old ladies. "We tend to knit jumpers, scarves and gloves," said another.

Reaching for some old strips of wood left in an old store cupboard at the back of the hall, Alexander quickly constructed a giant knitting machine that rapidly knitted a huge woollen jumper, leaving the little old ladies astonished. Whether they had any friends or relatives large enough to fit the giant woollen garment the machine produced was yet to be seen. But they were impressed, nonetheless.

One of the old ladies politely said, "This is simply amazing, but I'm not sure that people are quite this large. Could you adjust it a bit, so that it knits clothing that would fit people our size?"

After a few adjustments by Alexander, the knitting machine could make clothing of the appropriate size for regular sized humans.

Before long he had used it to create several jumpers and three beautiful hoodies that the little old ladies then put on over their normal clothing. "Ooh! I like this hoodie, it's ever so warm and cosy," said one of them.

"You look cool," said Alexander to the old ladies. "You hanging with the kids, girls!" Alexander playfully added. Alexander was proud to have switched the grannies from old fashioned cardigans and jumpers to starting to wear hoodies. And before he knew it they were racing across the village green to show them off to their friends selling jams and chutney.

Upon stepping back outside, Luna and Alexander found that the large crowd had dispersed, and that a degree of peace had returned to the village. They took this opportunity to have a better look at the country fair they had stumbled across, and unintentionally disrupted.

They soon spotted some food stalls selling a variety of things to eat. One stall offered homemade roast beef rolls, another smelled of a delicious Thai curry, while the third food stall sold pizza.

Without missing a beat, Alexander made a beeline for the pizza stall. He chose a large cheese and pepperoni pizza with an extra kick of chillies. Luna shook her head in mock disbelief, laughing.

Then Alexander purchased a Thai curry too and poured it onto the top of the pizza! Finally, in a single swift motion, Alexander reached up into a nearby tree, pulled out a fistful of woodlice and sprinkled them onto his pizza too, much to the surprise of the crowd that was forming.

Folding the pizza in half, Alexander popped the lot into his large gaping mouth and promptly gulped it down in a single mouthful.

Two teenage lads standing behind Alexander gasped and one proclaimed that Alexander was a "Legend!"

Fed, watered, and adored by the crowd, Luna and Alexander swiftly hopped back into the land vehicle that Alexander and Oscar had named 'DINO 1'. To avoid confusion, they had even stencilled this in big bold letters onto the doors of the craft.

However, just before they were about to leave, Alexander suddenly declared, "I just have to do one last thing!" Then, much to Luna's surprise, with a slight twitch of his nose, all the people at the village fair froze, their expressions now completely blank.

"What did you just do?" asked Luna with a quizzical look.

"I wiped their minds clear," answered Alexander, adding, "So they don't remember meeting me here today. It's one of my 'special powers'."

"Wow," exclaimed Luna, "How many powers do you have, Alexander? Do all dinosaurs have that power?"

"No, it is very rare. It is one of my very special powers. Not many Dinosaurs can do that at all. We can all disappear and we are all teleportic," announced Alexander with a grin.

"Telepathic, you mean," Luna correcting him, adding, "What other powers do you, dinosaurs, have then?"

"We can do all sorts, Luna. Some of us can read minds, others can smell an oil spill thousands of miles away. Some of us can even predict the future, which is very useful if you want to avoid dangerous situations," answered Alexander in a very matter-of-fact way.

Luna's mouth was wide open in amazement at this latest piece of news. Was there nothing these dinosaurs couldn't do?

Alexander put DINO 1 into gear and then drove it off at a high speed, along the winding country road, back towards the cave.

The sail at the back of the vehicle fluttered noisily, as they sped along in near silence.

"Alexander, do you think more people will start using vehicles like this in the future?" she asked.

Alexander nodded, his large head bobbing up and down. "I think so," he said. "As people become more aware of the damage that pollution is causing, they'll want to find new solutions. And vehicles like this one are a good way to turn a problem into a solution."

"It cleans up the environment and lets people go about their business carbon-free," he concluded.

Before arriving back home, they carefully stowed DINO 1 away in a small cave near to the main cave's entrance.

Luna looked across the bay and into the surrounding hills, marvelling at the natural beauty of the place. And then she stopped in her tracks. Once again, the same hatchet-faced man with the binoculars was there watching their every move.

She decided it was time to mention this to Oscar when she next had him to herself. Something highly suspicious was going on.

CHAPTER 12

Dino Power Inc is Born!

L una had begun to receive more and more emails from the world's media. The news had spread rapidly about Oscar and his horde of dinosaurs reappearing and their plans to save the Earth from climate change.

This had only been boosted further by Luna's trip to the country fair with Alexander, which was now all over social media. Even though Alexander had wiped clean the minds of the people in the village they visited, quite a few people had already posted pictures of a giant dinosaur with a tall blonde girl online.

When the media visited the small, picturesque village to find out more about the latest dinosaur sighting, none of the locals knew what the paparazzi were even talking about. Although the ladies of the local village committee were a little bemused at how they now had a fully functioning knitting machine in their possession and a new hoodie each, with a dinosaur image knitted into the hood.

The truth was that the media were eager for any news that related to the dinosaurs. And Luna realised now was an opportunity to share the message of Dino Power Inc and its mission to save the world with everyone.

Luna's enthusiasm knew no bounds when it came to getting publicity for the dinosaurs' cause. They would need to reach a global audience and gain support for their mission if they were to get worldwide support. It would also help stop Big Oil from snuffing out their movement before it even began.

After thinking long and hard, Luna decided that the best course of action now would be to organise a big press conference in London and maybe some of the other major cities of the world. To do this, she would need to rally the support of Oscar and some of the other dinosaurs. Luna hoped that they would agree to participate in this important event.

These kinds of interactions with humans unnerved Oscar, and from what Luna could gather, it stemmed from the events of the day they had met the President, before all the dinosaurs suddenly vanished.

When she finally presented her ideas to Oscar and the other dinosaurs, they were hesitant at first.

Oscar, with a sceptical look on his face, scratched his head with his short arms. "A press conference, Luna? You know humans can be a bit unpredictable. Last time we did something like that, it got pretty wild."

Alexander, always the voice of reason, chimed in, "Oscar's got a point. We've been doing great work without making a spectacle of ourselves. Why change things now? Can't we just take it slowly?"

Olivia, an ever optimistic orange-feathered dinosaur, bounced on her feet, "Oh, come on you lot! It'll be perfectly safe. We just tell them what we've been up to, and they'll love it!"

Hugo, who always had a more reserved approach to things, thought long and hard before speaking. "Publicity can be a double-edged sword. We need to ensure it helps, not hinders," he said.

Luna, undeterred, reminded them about their achievements so far, highlighting the incredible progress they had made as a team. From finding innovative ways to clean the oceans to inventing technology for clean and carbon-free renewable energy, they had already made a significant difference. She urged them that by sharing their knowledge with the world, they could play a vital role in fighting climate change.

"Think about it," Luna passionately continued. "We can inspire people, show them that there's hope and real solutions. Dino Power Inc can become a global symbol of positive change. The world needs to know what we're doing and what we stand for!"

Oscar, with a quizzical expression, turned to Olivia, who was able to see into the future and read minds, and asked, "So, Olivia, how are we looking on the safety front?"

Olivia, her eyes narrowing in concentration, replied, "I sense it's safe, but there's a twist. I see an angry-looking man with a strange and secret past. Weird, right?"

Oscar raised an eyebrow, "'Secret past? Sounds like trouble."

Despite this ominous glimpse into the future, Olivia reassured them, "I genuinely think it's safe to proceed with the press conference. Just keep an eye out for the man in the dark suit."

Luna, leaning forward, added with a smile, "No worries, Olivia. We'll have an invisible guard - our crew's 100 strongest dinosaurs. They'll be all around, unseen and ready to pounce if needed."

Oscar nodded, "Our security detail. Just in case."

Luna, feeling the need to give Oscar a bit more reassurance, said, "Don't worry Oscar. You can all just vanish in an instant if things get dicey."

Oscar chuckled, "True, Luna, but a little extra caution never hurt anyone. And we need to protect you too."

Gradually, with Luna's infectious enthusiasm and the trust they had in her, the dinosaurs warmed to the idea.

The dinosaurs exchanged glances, a silent conversation passing between them. After a thoughtful pause, Oscar finally nodded. "Alright, Luna. Let's give it a shot. But we do it our way, no compromises on our principles."

Luna beamed, "Of course Oscar! No compromises at all."

Astrid, the wise one, mused, "Well, I guess we better start practising our English and working on our presentations then, eh? It's time we step into the spotlight."

With everyone on board, they all began preparing for the press conference.

Luna typed furiously to write an invitation, outlining their mission to protect the Earth. She knew the world was eager to hear their story, and she was determined to share it with them.

She then sent out hundreds of emails inviting all the world's major newspapers and TV channels to the event, along with a very smart looking invitation to the press.

It read:

DINO POWER INC

Oscar the dinosaur and his friends have returned with an important mission: to save the Earth and all its inhabitants.

These remarkable creatures were discovered in the Appalachian Mountains, only to mysteriously disappear. Now they're back, with an urgent message for humanity: Change or face the consequences.

They have united to form Dino Power Inc. with a commitment to harness clean, renewable energy from the Earth's core. Their goal is to reduce our carbon footprint by developing sustainable technologies to remove pollution and plastics from our air, seas, and lands, and then recycling them into more renewable energy sources.

Every penny of profit generated will be directed toward charitable causes such as rainforest preservation, atmospheric damage repair, protecting endangered species, and cleaning up the world's oceans and waterways.

The dinosaurs are thrilled to be back and want to bring love and fun into our lives. They want to ensure that we are not the last humans to inhabit our beautiful planet. Their mission extends to protecting all Earth's creatures.

These lively dinosaurs adore having fun and sharing humour. They have quickly become avid fans of rap, hip hop, and online games. They love sharing pizza and jokes with their friends, even if their pizza toppings might seem a bit crazy for our tastes - but hey, they're dinosaurs!

This is your opportunity to meet Oscar and his friends in person and hear their message directly from them:

Drinks and pizza at 12:30 PM, press conference at 1:30 PM (strange dinosaur pizza toppings not compulsory).

Please feel free to bring a friend. Together, we can work toward a brighter, cleaner future.

RSVP

In no time at all, Luna's email inbox started to overflow with literally hundreds of acceptances to her invitations. The buzz surrounding the press conference was electric, and anyone who was anyone wanted to be part of this important event.

Luna realised that she needed to book a hotel - a really big one.

Luna soon found a stunning conference centre within a large hotel in London's Mayfair district, close to their office. It had enough space to host up to 500 people.

Luna spent the next few days preparing for the press conference. She put together a presentation about the remarkable carbon-free power technology the dinosaurs had invented. Her presentation detailed their plans and how this innovative technology would help to combat global warming.

She hoped that with the help of the world's media, they could spread the word about the importance of protecting the environment and show the world that dinosaurs were not just a thing of the past.

Before long, the big day arrived.

The conference centre was beautifully decorated with towering flower arrangements and grand crystal chandeliers that sparkled elegantly. Large screens displayed images of Oscar, Luna, and some of the other dinosaurs, including Alexander, Hugo and Astrid.

Luna stood confidently with Oscar at the podium on a grand stage within the conference centre. The room was packed with reporters, cameras flashing, and an atmosphere of eager anticipation.

Luna began to speak, "Our journey began with a remarkable discovery, the existence of these incredible dinosaurs who are not only my dear friends and companions but also champions of a more sustainable future. I've witnessed their determination to fight pollution, generate eco-friendly forms of power and to invent new ways for us to travel."

The reporters listened attentively, recording Luna's words on their devices, cameras flashing, mobile phones held up high, recording and videoing her every word.

Luna continued, "We stand at a critical crossroads where our choices can shape the destiny of our planet. The time to act is now, and these dinosaurs are here to remind us of the urgency of this situation and to demonstrate new ways to address the challenges we face."

Luna paused briefly for breath and then pressed on, "Their inventions will hopefully help us eliminate our dependence on fossil fuels within 10 years." They've shown us that we can discover solutions that protect our environment and benefit us all. We have the ability to create change and it begins with adopting sustainable practices."

Luna then brought her presentation to an inspirational end, "Now is the age of the Dinosaur. Now is the time for Dino Power!"

Applause and cheers erupted from the audience. It was clear that the dinosaurs' message resonated. The dinosaurs exchanged proud glances with Luna, who smiled back at them.

As Luna had spoken, a big film camera had panned over to Oscar, Alexander, Hugo, and Astrid, who stood by her side.

She then introduced Oscar and explained that he was the leader of the dinosaurs and the chief inventor of many of the innovations that she hoped would pave the way for a greener world.

Oscar then prepared to speak, gently blushing, tapping the microphone and saying, "Testing, testing."

"Hello everybody, I am pleased to speak to you today about our vision. Thanking you for coming."

The entire audience sat in astonishment, shocked to hear a talking dinosaur address them.

Oscar went on to explain their vision and talked about some of their groundbreaking inventions, or "vinentions," as Oscar called them, inviting a few chuckles from the audience.

Oscar passionately explained that things really didn't need to be how they were, emphasising that Dino Power could save people money, clean up the environment, and most importantly, save the planet.

The press conference was a complete success. Luna and the other dinosaurs spoke eloquently about their plans, their accomplishments, and their long-term dream for a more sustainable future.

The world's media buzzed with excitement. The dinosaurs were about to become global superstars, to be hailed as environmental heroes, the talk of London and the rest of the world.

More or less everyone who attended the press conference were lining up for selfies with Oscar, Alexander, Hugo and Astrid.

Except, that is, for one very strange - almost sinister - man in a dark suit, who remained silent throughout the entire press conference. He simply stood at the back, staring, which had an unsettling effect on Luna. Even Oscar, who is telepathic, couldn't quite understand the man's thoughts or intentions.

Was this the strange, angry-looking man that Olivia had warned them about?

Suddenly, the man leapt up, standing on an empty seat and screamed at Luna and Oscar with a loud, rude voice, he shouted at the top of his lungs, his voice cutting through the optimistic atmosphere of the event.

"This is all a hoax!" he bellowed, his words echoing around the room. "A complete and utter hoax!" He pointed an accusatory finger towards Luna, the dinosaurs, and the stage. "There are no such things as dinosaurs," he declared, his eyes burning with venomously. "And global warming is all made up. This is just a ridiculous publicity stunt. In fact, it is a scam!" the man added spitefully. "They are just very clever AI generated holograms," he concluded.

His outburst sent shockwaves through the room, and the audience fell into a stunned silence, their excitement from a few minutes ago now replaced by a terrible tension.

Luna felt her heart race as the man's words hung in the air, challenging everything she and the dinosaurs had worked so hard to convey.

Oscar, growing tired of the man's outburst, then quickly stepped forward and let out a mighty roar in his deep, booming voice. "You are wrong, sir," he declared with authority. "We are real enough. We were just waiting to be discovered for gonzillions of years deep in a cave. We are here now to help heal the damage done to the planet by you humans. We are back to share our knowledge and ideas with the world."

The man in the dark suit appeared visibly taken aback and slightly intimidated by Oscar's size and outburst. For a moment, he simply stared at Oscar, then began to quickly make his way toward the exit of the large hotel conference centre. Members of the audience buzzed with disbelief.

Luna felt a deep sense of pride and gratitude toward Oscar for his passionate defence.

The angry man quickly rushed off, sensing that his presence was no longer wanted and perhaps fearing for his own safety - from both the enraged press and the furious horde of dinosaurs.

Luna watched him climb into a big gas guzzling limousine that was sitting outside with the engine running. It was driven by the man with a hatchet face. The same man who had been watching her recently through his binoculars and had followed her that day she visited the bank in Swansea.

The incident with the strange angry man was fortunately the only dampener on the day. It was an unmistakable proof of Olivia's ability to see into the future. She had foreseen the angry man in the dark suit long before the event even took place, yet she knew he posed no real threat.

Almost instantly, the dinosaurs' message and images were being broadcast around the world. And the invitations for Luna and Oscar to appear on chat shows and news programmes all over the world started to pour in.

Luna had also arranged for a select group of media representatives to be flown by the dinosaurs to their cave hideaway from the event, all blindfolded for security reasons of course.

Once there, they would have the opportunity to witness some of the dino contraptions that Oscar and his friends had invented and built.

That evening, the scent of freshly baked pizza and the sweet fizz of cola filled the air, and rhythmic beats of hip-hop music started to play.

The after-party was now in full swing, and the atmosphere was electric. Multi-coloured beams from repurposed disco lights danced across the cave walls, casting vibrant patterns all around the cave. A long, rustic table stretched out, adorned with huge delicious-looking pizzas, each one topped with a variety of both crazy and relatively normal toppings that catered to both dinosaurs and humans alike.

Although one journalist did take a bite out of one with an avocado and sandfly topping by mistake, to everyone's amusement. He spat it out and looked a little green for the rest of the evening.

The dinosaurs moved gracefully among their guests from the media, their towering bodies dwarfing the humans, yet their manner gentle and welcoming.

Oscar and his dinosaur friends took centre stage, showing the small group of journalists their eco-friendly inventions.

Oscar flew several of the journalists out over the ocean in his airship. Oscar insisted on no photographs or filming.

"Sorry this is all top secret still," he told them.

One of the journalists tried to secretly take a few pictures of the flying craft. But Oscar just nudged the journalist's arm, causing him to drop his phone into the deep ocean below. Nobody else dared to try taking a sneaky picture of Oscar's airship after that.

Laughter and conversation filled the cave, as members of the world's press mingled with several hundred dinosaurs.

All in all, it was a great day for Dino Power!

CHAPTER 13

The World Tour

Driven by the success of the London press conference and several other similar events in New York, Tokyo, Sydney, Singapore, Hong Kong, and Paris, Oscar and the other dinosaurs became some of the most well-known celebrities on Earth.

With Dino Power skyrocketing in popularity, it seemed like everyone wanted a piece of the action. Oscar and his dino buddies were suddenly in very high demand.

Amid the glitz and glamour of their newfound celebrity status, Luna couldn't contain her excitement. "Oscar," she beamed, "you do realise you're like the coolest celebrity and the most famous dinosaur on the planet right now!"

Oscar, true to his nature, maintained his laid-back manner. He grinned at Luna, responding, "Well, you know Luna, being a famous dinosaur wasn't on my to-do list but I'm not going to fight it if it helps save the earth."

As they navigated the whirlwind of interviews and meetings, Luna couldn't help but tease him, "You're not going to those high-profile meetings dressed like that, are you?" She gestured to Oscar's usual daytime attire - a hoodie and a baseball cap.

Oscar winked, "Of course! Keeps things interesting. Besides, who says a dinosaur can't have some street cred and a bit of style?"

Luna chuckled at his laid back attitude to life, appreciating the fun and humour he brought to just about every situation.

Amid the laughter, Luna admired Oscar's ability to balance humour with a serious commitment to their cause. She noticed that despite his fame, he held very high standards. There were offers from big corporations, but Oscar simply turned down those that didn't align with their mission to protect the environment and sustainability.

In fact, a couple of major corporations tried to buy up the global rights to the new Dino Power technology, but Oscar, with his telepathic abilities, saw through their intentions. He knew they would buy up the rights to the technology and then not take the new idea forward.

"Some of these folks," Oscar confided in Luna, "were trying to buy Dino Power and all my inventions, but my telepathic powers told me they'd just kill it all off to help protect their huge profits from selling carbon fuels like oil and gas. They didn't really want change, just to stop us in our mission."

Luna, Oscar, along with Alexander, Hugo and Astrid, embarked on a world tour to generate even more publicity for the Dino Power movement. They appeared in TV interviews in just about every language imaginable, from Chinese and Yiddish to Bengali and Spanish. Oscar and his dinosaur buddies could speak almost every language that there is, which astonished audiences everywhere.

They met the Dalai Lama. The Dalai Lama, known for his wisdom and compassionate teachings, welcomed Oscar and Luna warmly into his presence. He shared insights on harmony, mindfulness, and the interconnectedness of all life, leaving a profound impact on them both.

Luna couldn't believe her luck when she found out the Dalai Lama had never tried pizza before. She gasped, "You've never tried pizza? Not at all? We need to fix this, like, immediately!"

Her eyes sparkled with mischief as she hatched a plan. "How about a pizza party? Oscar, imagine the Dalai Lama trying our favourite dino dish!"

Oscar, always up for a good time, replied, "Count me in! I've always wanted to see a spiritual leader tackle a slice of pepperoni pizza - American Hot."

The Dalai Lama, with a serene smile, agreed to Luna's quirky idea. "Pizza party it is! But remember, I'm vegetarian every other day, so let's not create a spiritual stir."

Luna, with a mischievous grin, teased, "Don't worry, we've got enough veggies to make a tomato blush."

The gang trooped to a nearby pizzeria, where Luna had meticulously planned a pizza party fit for a spiritual leader and a gang of hungry dinosaurs.

"I never thought I'd see the day when I'm deciding between pineapple and olives for the Dalai Lama," Luna chuckled as she scrutinised the menu.

Oscar chimed in, "Just don't ask him if pineapple belongs on pizza. We might start an international incident."

Luna and Oscar had decorated the room for a pirate-themed party, and she wasn't sure how the Dalai Lama would react to it. She had bought inflatable decorations in a variety of fun shapes suitable for this theme. Luna felt particularly proud of the inflatable palm tree tucked in one corner and an inflatable treasure chest placed in another corner.

The dinosaurs brandished wooden cutlasses and wore black eye patches.

The pizzas arrived, a colourful mosaic of flavours to suit every taste. Luna, eager to impress the Dalai Lama, declared, "Your Holiness, may I present the pizza extravaganza?"

As they ate the pizza, Luna glanced nervously at the inflatable decorations. "What do you think of the palm tree, Your Holiness? It's for a treasure island vibe."

The Dalai Lama, with a twinkle in his eye, replied, "I find it quite enlightening. Much like the wisdom of the Buddha swaying in the breeze."

Oscar, trying hard not to snort, whispered to Luna, "Looks like our inflatable decor passed the spiritual test."

In between bites of pizza and philosophical musings, the Dalai Lama shared profound insights on compassion and environmental stewardship.

"I try to treat whoever I meet as an old friend. This gives me a genuine feeling of happiness. It is the practice of compassion," the Dali Lamar told Luna. "In today's materialistic society, if you have money and power, you seem to have many friends. But they are not friends of yours; they are the friends of your money and power," he continued. "By the way I love the pirate outfits," he concluded.

Luna, beaming, thought, "Who knew a pirate-themed pizza party could be so spiritually enlightening?"

As their world tour continued, Oscar and Luna also met a very famous middle-aged rock star at a big climate conference in Switzerland.

Oscar couldn't help but raise an eyebrow at the rock star's actions. When the rock star arrived at their climate change meeting, it was in a huge limousine that gleamed under the streetlights. He hid his enormous car around the corner and the rock star then strolled in claiming he had come on the bus.

"Hey Luna," Oscar whispered. "Did you see that limo? It was so big, it could probably fit a whole herd of dinosaurs inside of it!"

Later, when the climate conference ended, Oscar and Luna followed him, flying high in the sky, as he made his way back in the huge limousine to a waiting private jet. Its engines roared into life the moment the strange rock star arrived on the tarmac runway and the rock star flew off back to Ireland, alone in the huge jet.

When he saw the rock star's private jet revving its engines, Oscar couldn't resist a remark. "I guess he's not really quiet on board with the whole 'save the planet' thing," he quipped.

This said, and despite Oscar's reservations about the rock star's choice of transportation, the meeting Oscar had with him proved to be highly productive. Oscar's commitment to carbon-free energy left a lasting impression on the rock star. He offered to use his influence to help spread the dinosaurs' message to all his fans and followers.

In a light-hearted moment, the rock star even confessed to enjoying a slice of pizza from time to time. However, despite loving a wide range of toppings, he drew the line at trying one with crushed fireflies, even if it was one of Oscar's favourite toppings.

Luna giggled. "Well, at least he's got some taste," she teased.

Luna and Oscar continued their mission by meeting with environmental activists, scientists, and political leaders. They shared their incredible story and tirelessly spread awareness about the need for sustainable energy and shared some of their innovative new ideas about creating renewable energy.

Luna and Oscar, the dynamic dino duo, were on a mission like no other. They didn't just conquer caves, they conquered hearts and minds too. Their journey led them to meet with a colourful cast of characters - environmental activists, scientists, and even a few political leaders.

Luna, with her boundless enthusiasm, exclaimed, "Oscar, you're turning into celebrity dinosaur superstar! Move over Hollywood, here comes Dino-wood!"

Oscar chuckled, "Well, I always knew my charm would come in handy one day. Who knew it would involve saving the planet!"

Their many meetings with the great and the good were like a comedy show mixed with a TED talk on renewable energy. Oscar, being the charismatic speaker he was, would often throw in a joke or two, just to keep things light.

Addressing a room full of global big shots at the United Nations, where Oscar had to wear a suit and a tie, Oscar couldn't resist a playful jab, "You know, folks, being a dinosaur in a suit feels a bit like a T-Rex trying to fit into a phone booth. But hey, if it gets the message across, I'll do it!"

The room erupted in laughter and applause.

Oscar then took a more serious turn, sharing a personal revelation. "When I first realised all my dinosaur ancestors had died millions of years ago, it hit me harder than a meteor. I thought, 'Well, that's a real downer'. But then Luna here came along."

Luna, wide-eyed, chimed in, "Yeah, and suddenly we became this oddball family of very special dinosaurs and me. I mean, who'd have thought?"

Oscar winked, "And here we are, trying to make sure Luna's world doesn't end up like ours did. Talk about dino deja vu!"

Their message resonated deeply, and Luna realised something profound. "You guys aren't just my buddies; you're like my guardians. It's like having a gang of overgrown, scaly, and feathery big brothers and sisters!"

Oscar, with a twinkle in his eye, replied, "Well, someone's got to keep you out of trouble, Luna. Might as well be a bunch of ancient, pizza-loving, eco-friendly dinosaurs, right?"

And so, the laughter and applause echoed through the halls of the United Nations, a reminder that even in the face of serious challenges, a sense of humour and a whole lot of heart can change the world.

After finishing their official meetings with politicians, celebrities, and TV hosts, Luna was surprised when Oscar suggested taking her on a trip around the world. He promised to show her new and exciting places she had never seen before.

In the following weeks, Luna and Oscar soared over mountains, across oceans, and through bustling cities. They visited ancient temples, glided over lush rainforests, and explored peaceful, deserted, white-sand beaches.

While flying through the skies, Luna couldn't help but notice the ways in which humans had damaged the world around them. Over Spain, she observed vast stretches of plastic greenhouses, blanketing the land and creating an unsettling, artificial landscape.

As they travelled along the Amazon, Luna's heart ached at the sight of once-beautiful rainforests torn apart to make way for more profitable crops. She witnessed how this destruction had disrupted the delicate balance of the ecosystem and she understood that the consequences would linger for years to come.

Despite the sadness she felt at seeing these changes, Luna remained hopeful. She believed that humans were capable of making a difference and finding solutions to these complex problems.

During this time, Oscar explained sustainable farming practices, conservation efforts, and various ways people were working to protect the environment to Luna. She soon understood that even simple actions, like recycling and conserving water, could have a positive impact when everyone played their part.

She began to realise that, as Oscar had once explained to her when he was very young, dinosaurs might just be more intelligent than humans.

As they travelled the world, Luna observed that Oscar was right. More and more people were becoming aware of the consequences of climate change and the pressing need for action. She took pride in the role that she and the dinosaurs were playing in raising awareness and inspiring change.

And then, one day, she gazed out from Oscar's back and saw a sprawling mountain range that seemed vaguely familiar.

A sudden spark of recognition lit up Luna's eyes. They were back in the Appalachian Mountains, quite close to the spot where Luna and Noah had originally found Oscar and the other dinosaurs.

Oscar grinned mischievously as they touched down in the Appalachian Mountains. "We are gonna stop here for lunch, Luna," he announced with a twinkle in his eye.

Luna, her hair windswept from their globe-trotting adventure, laughed. "Finally, back where it all started with the most fabulous pink dinosaur in the world!"

Oscar landed with a thud, startling a few local farmers who stared wide-eyed at the enormous pink phenomenon in their backyard. In a flash, Oscar turned invisible, leaving the farmers scratching their heads and eyeing their moonshine whiskey with suspicion.

One of the farmers drawled to his friend, "I swear, Jed, I'm sure I just saw a giant pink dinosaur right over there!"

Jed, squinting at the now-empty spot, replied, "Must be the moonshine talkin'. Let's pour the rest out, don't wanna be havin' dinosaur-inducing hallucinations. Think this latest batch o' moonshine is no good."

As Luna and Oscar enjoyed their invisible picnic together, Luna's eyes sparkled.

"Oscar! This is where we discovered you and the gang!"

Oscar nodded, a twinge of nostalgia showing in his bright, beautiful dinosaur eyes. "Yup, right here in the Appalachians. Feels like a gonzillion years ago now though."

Luna chuckled, "Well, you haven't aged a bit, Oscar!"

Oscar laughed, taking a theatrical bow. "Thank you, thank you. Being fabulous is a full-time job!"

As they savoured their pizza, Luna marvelled at the journey they'd taken, "From the UN to the Amazon, and now back to where it all began."

Oscar, munched away on his prune and peanut butter pizza with all the elegance of a pizza connoisseur, replied, "Well, Luna, life is an adventure. And what's an adventure without a bit of dinosaur magic and a whole lot of fun and laughter?"

Luna laughed, "You're right, Oscar. This has been the craziest, most fantastic journey ever!"

Oscar, with a bright glint in his eyes, declared, "And it's far from over, Luna. The world is our oyster, and there's still so much more to do."

As they soared back into the sky once again, Luna couldn't help but feel grateful for the laughter, the magic, and the unmistakable joy of having a pink dinosaur as her travel buddy.

Oscar then landed quietly in a small woodland clearing nearby, opposite a steep rocky cliff face.

Oscar quickly scanned the surroundings, ensuring no one was watching. Once he was confident the coast was clear, he swiftly darted into a hidden, narrow, stone passageway and Luna followed.

Eventually, they reached a dead-end, blocked by a massive round rock. Oscar tapped rhythmically on it, about 20 times, in a very specific pattern. "Tip, tap, tappetty, tip, tap, tap tip, tippet!", he tapped. And then, as if by magic, the large smooth rock rolled quietly and smoothly over to one side, to reveal the North American offices of Dino Power Inc.

A group of dinosaurs rushed forward to greet Luna and Oscar, their surprise and excitement evident. At the back of the hollowed-out cavern, a tall, young man stood. Luna's heart leaped with joy - it was Noah! His dark, wiry, coiled hair was longer now, and he was dressed in trendy streetwear.

He stood there with a warm, broad smile on his face. Noah appeared noticeably older than the last time Luna had seen him, this time exuding a newfound sense of confidence. He walked up to Luna and Oscar, looking like a young CEO of a Silicon Valley tech startup.

Luna, trying to keep her cool, said with a smile to Oscar, "Is this the Dino Power HQ of North America? Or a hipster dinosaur club?"

Oscar winked, "Why not both?"

At first, Noah started to extend his hand out for a formal handshake. However, before anyone could react properly, the trio found themselves in a massive group hug. "Ahhh it's so good to see you, guys!" Noah exclaimed.

Pizza boxes materialised out of nowhere, and Luna, Noah, and Oscar found themselves feasting on New York style pizza. Oscar, playing DJ with his tail, cranking up the latest hip-hop beats.

Luna, a pizza slice in hand, nodded to Noah. "So, what's happening Noah?"

Noah, Oscar and Luna talked for hours about everything they had achieved so far and their plans for the future. Noah confided in Luna, expressing increasing worries about Big Oil. He shared that he had received some unsettling threats from a mysterious figure named Dr. Carbon.

"Big Oil is getting very angry about what we are doing. Some guy named Dr. Carbon is sending us threatening emails. He says we're spreading false information about climate change and that the dinosaurs aren't real."

Luna, gasped, "Dr. Carbon? Seriously? He sounds like the villain in a zombie horror story or something."

Noah feared that there was a real possibility of Dr. Carbon sabotaging their technology and putting them out of business.

Noah shrugged. "More like a dino-hating mastermind with a keyboard. He could mess up all our hard work and plans if we aren't careful, Luna. We need to discover who he is and what he plans to do."

Luna wasn't sure how to respond. She knew that finding the dinosaurs and their hidden caves wouldn't be easy for Dr. Carbon, let alone attempting to sabotage their turbines and other secret inventions tucked away deep within their cave systems.

And then Luna remembered the hatchet-faced man who had been spying on her, who drove the angry man in the dark suit away from the London press conference.

She decided it was time to talk to Oscar and Noah about them. Perhaps one of these two sinister men was Dr. Carbon.

Luna, with a glint of determination, said, "You remember those two guys from the conference in London, right? The hatchet-faced one and the angry one?"

Noah and Oscar exchanged glances before Oscar rumbled, "Yeah, I remember those shady characters. What about them?"

Luna leaned in, "I think one of them might be Dr. Carbon. One of them has been watching me, whenever I leave or arrive back at the cave in Wales. I think it is time for us all to do some detective work to find out what is really going on here!"

They all agreed they needed to work out how they could track down Dr. Carbon and start to find out what he planned.

Noah asked Oscar if he would take him and Luna for a quick flight around the area, before they left.

Oscar soared through the sky like a prehistoric super hero, carrying both Luna and Noah and travelling at an incredible speed. He even broke the sound barrier, with a loud "crack."

Noah, enjoying the ride, shouted over the wind, "Oscar, you're faster than a hypersonic pterodactyl! How do you do it?"

Oscar, an invisible grin audible in his voice, replied, "Trade secret, Noah. A dinosaur never reveals his secrets!"

As they touched down back at Noah's cave to drop him off before they left for home, Luna hugged Noah. "You gotta visit us in Wales, Noah. We have the best caves there, I promise!"

Noah chuckled, "Count on it, Luna. Your cave is on my all-time caving bucket list!"

After many months of globe-trotting, Oscar and Luna finally cruised back across the Atlantic towards the English coast. Luna, peering over Oscar's invisible back, marvelled at the ocean liners cutting through rough waters below. "Look at those ships, Oscar!" she yelled. "I bet they don't have a DJ like you on board."

"Or shooting stars as entertainment!" Oscar replied, looking up at the ink black, star-spangled sky.

Luna, pretending to reach out for the stars like a cosmic catcher, laughed, "I'm going to collect a few shooting stars for our light show back at our cave. It's gonna be epic!"

As they approached the Welsh coast near their cave, Luna spotted the rocky cliffs of home growing larger and larger.

Then, they soared over the steep cliff face in the darkness, startling two men sea fishing who were almost asleep. Oscar flew just a few feet above their heads, whisking their hats off into the sea in the process.

Luna giggled, "Oops! I hope they can swim. They'll need to if they want to get their hats back."

Both Oscar and Luna were tired when they arrived home, but they were happy knowing they had made a difference to the world and had got their movement really underway with millions of fans and followers. They had successfully spread their message and rallied thousands of people to join their mission to change the way the world works. The Dino Power movement was gaining momentum but there was still a lot to do.

"Yay. Home sweet cave!" Luna cheered.

Luna quickly fell asleep soundly in her hammock that night with a huge smile on her face, dreaming of a cleaner and more sustainable future for everyone.

CHAPTER 14

Dr. Carbon and His Filth Bots

It was 10 minutes past midnight, yet Dr. Carbon was still working away tirelessly from an abandoned airfield on the south coast of the Isle of Wight. It was the centre of his sinister empire and it oozed with darkness and spiteful greed.

Dr. Carbon, not so much evil as just plain greedy, was on a mission to protect Big Oil's interests and to destroy Dino Power in the process.

He worked relentlessly towards this goal, day and night, from a large, run-down, single-story Nissan hut, located at the centre of the old, dilapidated airfield. He liked the privacy that this location offered him, letting him carry out his work undetected by the media or the authorities.

His work included spreading rumours and false information about pollution and climate change on social media. This involved creating endless social media posts with apparent "experts" claiming that climate change was simply a hoax and that the planet had actually been warming up for thousands of years. He did this to confuse people and to mislead them.

Sometimes, Dr. Carbon couldn't spread rumours about inventions that might help reduce our reliance on gas and oil emerged quickly enough. People saw the value of these new inventions before he could influence them with his lies. If this happened, he would buy full control of the new inventions with the millions given to him by Big Oil. Once he had full control, he would immediately squash the inventions, making sure they never saw the light of day.

Dr. Carbon was paid generously for his work by Big Oil, normally in large gold bars. "Gold is best, better than money in the bank," he would say. He kept his enormous gold stash in a giant steel safe at the back of his shabby hut. The safe itself was almost as high as the roof of the hut, 12 metres wide and about two metres deep. And it was very, very full of big, heavy gold bars.

Dr Carbon sat in his dimly lit lair, muttering as he worked. He muttered about Luna. He muttered about Oscar the dinosaur. And he muttered about Noah.

On the walls of his hut were large photographs of well-known eco-activists. Each had the crosshairs of a gun sight aimed at their heads (drawn roughly in big, thick, black pen), as if an assassin were poised to pull the trigger. Among these many pictures, there was one of Luna, one of Oscar, and a third of Noah.

His hut echoed with his mutterings. "Mutter, mutter, let's crush their ideas. Silence their voices. Keep the world hooked on carbon fuels," he whispered to himself, a dark smile playing on his thin, tight lips. "Greed is good," he told his computer screen, as if it was an old friend.

A large moth fluttered around his desk, banging into the light shade above Dr. Carbon noisily, attracted by the large light that illuminated his coffee stained, dusty desk.

"Mutter, mutter, Luna's eco-influence. Can't let it grow," he grumbled, eyes darting to the portraits on his wall. Among the crosshairs and sinister portraits, Luna, Oscar, and Noah stared back, all targets on Dr. Carbon's hit list.

"Luna. That meddling girl! Hmppf! And that daft pink dinosaur. Think they can change the world? Not on my watch," he complained bitterly.

"Mutter, mutter, Noah," he sneered, scrolling through his emails. "Thinks he can outsmart the big oil corporations. We'll soon see about that."

The main building of Dr. Carbon's lair was a nondescript, grey structure with grimy windows and a round, asbestos curved roof, which was covered in moss.

It housed long rows of old steel filing cabinets, full of papers and dog-eared documents, and banks of big, dirty, desktop computers that had seen better days. They were all jam-packed full of evidence of a long-term conspiracy by Big Oil to stop anyone ever threatening their destructive money-making ways.

A stale, acrid smell permeated everything. The stench drifted into every nook and cranny, impregnating the walls, the ceilings and the ripped, shabby curtains that hung in some of the windows. Nothing had ever been cleaned, or polished or wiped for decades. Most people wouldn't have been able to work in this revolting environment but yet Dr. Carbon seemed to relish the filth and the smells. He found them familiar and reassuring.

In some of the other buildings, scattered around this defunct, shabby airfield, Dr. Carbon ran one of the largest troll farms in the world, to make sure his misleading messages swamped any positive messages online.

A troll farm, for those of you that don't know, is a facility that just creates thousands and thousands of false social media posts to influence public opinion. Sometimes this is done by computers that have been pre-programmed to do this automatically, sometimes it is done by actual people working day and night. Dr. Carbon had both.

In one building, there were hundreds of computer terminals that spread tens of thousands of malicious social media posts every day. Many of them rubbishing what Oscar and Luna had been doing and even claiming that the dinosaurs didn't really exist - saying that they were simply very clever holograms.

The automated systems hummed day and night, running complicated computer programmes, spreading endless misinformation. Rows and rows of computers, arranged like silent soldiers, executing their pre-programmed orders with cold precision.

The exterior of the building that housed all this was weather-beaten, the windows dirty, betraying none of the sinister activity going on inside.

Dr. Carbon also owned an old trawler boat, complete with peeling blue paint and layers of crusty barnacles. He used this boat to intercept migrants trying to cross the English Channel from France. These hopeful souls believed that they had been rescued by the English authorities, but the harsh reality of their fate dawned on them too late. They were forced into joining Dr. Carbon's slave workforce, working 16-hour shifts every day, seven days a week. In exchange for this, they were given a small bowl of food each day and very little money - not that they could ever leave the island to spend it.

Dr. Carbon's enslaved workforce slept in row-upon-row of cheap bunk beds that had seen better days, with stained and broken mattresses and dirty covers and torn blankets. There was no running water for them apart from a single cold water tap outside. This only provided them with freezing cold drinking water, so they had to wash in the sea.

To supplement their meagre rations, they collected nettles to make weak tea, and seaweed to fry over a basic stove they had found in one of the smaller storage buildings.

These kidnapped migrants sat behind bank-upon-bank of dirty, old desk computers for hours on end. Their role: to flood social media platforms with thousands of messages daily, discrediting claims of global warming and rising sea levels.

Dr. Carbon even maintained a dedicated team whose only purpose was to spread the idea that the dinosaurs were a hoax. They created images using Photoshop showing they were nothing but holograms. They also spread the lie that Luna was a fraud, funded by her parents, who stood to profit from Dino Power as an online influencer. Fake news was the order of the day.

"Work faster, you pixel peasants!" Dr. Carbon barked, his old trawler boat bobbing about violently in the stormy sea behind him.

The migrants found themselves imprisoned on Dr. Carbon's airfield, surrounded by the sea on one side and tall barbed wire fences on the other, with no escape in sight. The work was gruelling, just sitting in front of a computer screen all day, their strength draining with each passing moment, with every tap of their sore fingers on their filthy keyboards - undernourished and half worked to death.

But all this wasn't enough for Dr. Carbon. He also had a team of powerful, smokey, oil powered robots known as Filth Bots. These oil-powered mischief-makers flitted around the globe, leaving trails of thick smoke, pollution and chaos behind them.

Dr. Carbon used the Filth Bots to sabotage any efforts to create clean energy. His ultimate goal was to prevent anyone from discovering new sources of power that could harm the oil industry's profits. And if they did, he would quickly snuff them out, or ruin their reputation. Often the Filth Bots would fire their rockets and destroy the clean energy devices.

"Filth Bots, my mechanical minions, find those generators!" Dr. Carbon ordered, a sinister gleam in his eyes, "Let's bury those dinosaurs and that girl, once and for all."

What Dr. Carbon didn't realise though, as the Filth Bots darted across various continents, leaving chaos in their wake, Luna, Oscar, and their allies were already gearing up for the ultimate showdown with him.

Dr. Carbon might have his isolated, polluted airfield, his captive workers, and his army of Filth Bots, but the dinosaurs had something more potent. They had unity, resilience, and a few surprises hidden up their scaly (or in the case of Oscar, feathery) sleeves. The battle for a cleaner, greener world was about to get underway big time!

CHAPTER 15

The Battle to Save Earth

One morning, after another night of playing online games, feasting on pizza, and jamming to some amazing hip hop sounds, Oscar went outside of the cave to get some fresh air. This was something of a daily ritual for Oscar. He did this most mornings after breakfast.

On this occasion, as Oscar hopped out of the secret cave entrance, he noticed a strange, smoking robot that was letting out plumes of rancid, black smoke, polluting the beautiful Welsh countryside. Oscar couldn't help but feel alarmed, fully aware of the grave dangers that pollution posed to the environment and the creatures that call it home.

He approached the robot cautiously and called out, "Hey, you there! What do you think you are doing? What's with the filthy smoke show, dude?" Oscar bellowed.

153

The robot, who introduced itself as Filth Bot 11, replied coldly, "I'm here to snuff out your Dino Power nonsense. Dr. Carbon says it's a threat to the oil industry. We don't take kindly to that."

Oscar was taken aback. He had never heard such greed, selfishness, and utter arrogance from anyone, let alone a smoke spewing robot. He also noticed that the Bot was armed with some lethal looking rockets up its sleeves, housed in its stumpy metal arms. He approached the Bot with caution, ready to disappear quickly if he needed to.

Oscar, bewildered by the robot's pre-programmed greed, argued, "We need solutions that benefit everyone, not just the rich."

The Filth Bot scoffed, "Profit is king. You can't stop us. Others have tried. None have succeeded."

Furious at this, Oscar whacked the robot into silence with one of his mighty wings and disabled it altogether. He left it there on the grass, spewing smoke, fizzing and whirring in the open field, for everyone to see.

Oscar then went invisible with a pop and decided to keep a close watch on the Filth Bot, to see if anyone came to retrieve it.

Oscar realised this might be the lucky break they had all been hoping for. It could help them find out where Dr. Carbon was based, if someone came to collect the Filth Bot. Once they knew where Dr. Carbon was located, they could then watch him to see what he was really up to.

Days passed, and just as Oscar was starting to lose hope that anyone would ever come, a very dirty, smoky helicopter landed on the grass next to the Filth Bot.

Then, to Oscar's astonishment, the angry man in the dark suit from the London press conference got out of the smoke-churning helicopter. He still looked angry.

As the man approached the robot, Oscar noticed something very peculiar. The man appeared to be talking to himself and making exaggerated hand gestures as he walked, as though he were having a heated argument with himself.

Oscar, completely invisible, moved closer to the man, and eavesdropped on his animated conversation. He discovered the man was arguing with an unseen voice on a mobile phone headset. And Oscar could hear every word of the conversation.

The voice on the other end was urging the man to continue his mission of protecting the interests of the oil industry and "To kill all those dinosaurs and that stupid young, know-it-all girl, Luna."

The angry man appeared furious as he roughly loaded the damaged robot into the helicopter and swiftly flew off with it, muttering away to himself.

Oscar kept out of sight, snarling a low growl. The battle against Dr. Carbon was escalating, and the dinosaurs were in the crosshairs of a sinister plan.

Determined to unearth the truth and protect his friends, he kept himself invisible and secretly trailed the dark-suited man in his helicopter to the heart of Dr. Carbon's villainous lair.

Eventually, the man arrived at his isolated airfield. The man landed his helicopter and vanished into a mysterious, drab building, dragging the disabled Filth Bot with him. Oscar, cautiously approached and carefully peeked through a window. Oscar listened to more of the heated argument between the angry man in the dark suit and the shadowy figure on the other end of the phone.

The shadowy voice urged, "Continue your mission, Dr. Carbon. Protect the interests of Big Oil, destroy those damn dinosaurs, and that meddlesome girl too. We are relying on you Carbon. Don't fail us."

Oscar now knew for sure that the angry mad man in the dark suit was Dr. Carbon. He also knew now, without doubt, where he was based.

Oscar's eyes widened, as he continued to listen to the sinister dialogue. "Too much at stake. Trillions of dollars in profits every year, just to save a few dolphins and polar bears! Get a grip, man!"

"Their inventions are far too clever, we are ruined if they go into widespread production," the voice continued.

Having heard enough, Oscar swiftly raced back to the cave to share the news with Luna and the other dinosaurs.

Oscar realised they would have to act fast.

In hushed tones, Oscar relayed the sinister plan and the urgency of the situation. Luna's eyes widened with concern as she grasped the gravity of the threat.

"What are we going to do, Oscar?" Luna asked, with a worried look in her eyes.

Oscar, brimming with determination, declared, "We fight back. And we win."

"It's time for battle stations," announced Oscar. "Dinosaurs stick to full stealth mode from now on. Remain invisible outside of the cave at all times. This man is dangerous. He wishes us all extreme harm!"

"I'm going to allocate ten of the strongest dinosaurs to stay here at the cave, with Luna, as her personal bodyguard. And no arguing Luna. I need you here to coordinate everything and I need you safe."

Oscar was determined and really started to shine through as the true leader he had always been.

"20 of our best water dinosaurs need to patrol the coast here. Then 25 need to get to the coast where Dr. Carbon's lair is, and quickly, to make sure he can't escape by boat," Oscar continued. "We need air cover here too, so let's have 20 invisible flying dinosaurs in the air around the cave, keeping watch day and night. Don't allow anyone, or anything, suspicious near to the cave - under any circumstances. We need to both protect and attack," Oscar concluded.

Within an hour, Oscar had dispatched 52 of his most skilled air dinosaurs back to the airfield to keep watch - fully invisible, of course, at all times.

"Remember to keep reporting back on a regular basis," Oscar requested. "I want to know everything as it happens."

The dinosaurs took turns watching, listening, and observing the actions and words of Dr. Carbon, his Filth Bots and his enslaved migrant workforce.

Dr. Carbon was completely oblivious that he had been rumbled and was being very carefully watched by a large group of invisible dinosaurs. Although Hugo did clumsily knock over an overfilled dustbin at one point, which made Dr. Carbon look up from his constant muttering and typing at one stage. But he thought little of it, muttering, "Probably just rats!"

And little did he know that the waters near his hideaway were being patrolled by a large invisible amphibious task force of aquatic dinosaurs too.

Every few hours, several of the dinosaurs that Oscar had sent to keep watch returned with a full report of what they had found out so far and received further orders from Oscar.

Liam, the leader of the air squadron of flying dinosaurs, had discovered that the Filth Bots had located the dinosaurs' secret cave network in the Welsh mountains and were plotting to blow up the entrance, trapping Luna, Oscar and the other dinosaurs inside. It seemed that Dr. Carbon had enough explosives to do this and was trying to hire a military helicopter and a small mercenary force of retired soldiers to pull this off. A cache of explosives was already hidden in a rocky area around the cliff face near to their cave, underneath a pile of rocks.

Oscar and Hugo went to investigate this and soon found the explosives. They quickly deactivated them and dropped them into the sea close to the cave to make sure that they couldn't be used.

Dr Carbon had by all accounts also planned to do the same at the North American Headquarters where Noah was based. It had just taken longer to pull everything together than Dr Carbon had expected, thank goodness.

Luna called Noah to warn him, so that he could ensure that his headquarters and all the dinosaurs who lived there were safe too. A global red alert was issued to all the dinosaurs' caves.

Armed with this latest information, Oscar, Hugo and a squadron of the most powerful flying dinosaurs then set out to capture Dr. Carbon and bring him back to their cave for questioning. The dinosaurs prepared a secure cell, deep within the cave complex, to make sure he couldn't escape once they had him in their custody.

Gliding through the air like a squadron of stealth fighter aircraft the group of dinosaurs, led by Oscar, closed in on their unsuspecting target. Their movements were as silent as whispers in the wind.

In a flash of coordinated precision, they descended upon Dr. Carbon, to capture him and to disable his Filth Bots before he could work out what was even happening.

With his magnificent strong wings and powerful talons, Oscar swept Dr. Carbon off his feet in a single, violent flash of pure pink. In a split second Oscar was swiftly carrying him away - back to the Welsh coast and to the depths of the dinosaurs' hidden cave.

Dr Carbon struggled and screamed and then muttered all the way. He shouted at Oscar, "Who do you think you are? You can't do this to me, you stupid dinosaur. Do you know who I am? I am personal friends of several Presidents and Prime Ministers...put me down...this instant. I'll report you... you monster!"

Oscar just ignored his endless protests and continued at top speed to back their cave.

The other flying dinosaurs then descended on the Filth Bots, who were now running around the airfield in alarm, firing their small rockets from their short stumpy arms in every direction.

The battle was really starting to hot up, but without Dr. Carbon's orders the Bots were a bit lost on how to respond to the continuous attack by the powerful squadron of invisible flying dinosaurs that continued to circle and dive without pausing for a single second.

The dinosaurs' sharp talons pierced the steel casings of the robots' bodies, cutting into the steel like a hot knife through butter. They snatched the smoking robots into the sky and dumped them into the deep ocean, where they were then watched closely by Asrid and her crew.

Hugo was particularly active, grabbing one after another of the Filth Bots. Swooping low, and then soaring off towards the big bright moon, with his prey dangling from his invisible claws. Silent, stealthy and relentless.

Hundreds of rockets were fired high into the sky by the Filth Bots, in the hope of hitting one of the many invisible flying dinosaurs swooping in and out of the disused airfield.

There were several loud squeals and flashes in the sky as one of two of the rockets hit their mark. Astrid stood on shore and watched this dramatic firework display, worried that one of her friends might have been badly injured, or worse!

The battle raged for more than two hours with over 176 Filth Bots being destroyed and dumped out at sea. Astrid then supervised them being retrieved from the sea once she knew they were completely disabled and could no longer do any harm. The wreckage was all piled up by the main hut at the airfield for Oscar to inspect later and to recycle parts where possible. 73 other Filth Bots hissed and fizzed on the ground, smoking violently, as the last gasp of their artificial life left them.

A couple of the returning air dino squadron had suffered slight burns and singed feathers from the rockets that had been fired by the Filth Bots. But Hugo was missing. Astrid and the others at the airfield started to worry about him.

Astrid and five of her water dinosaur fleet started to search the surrounding ocean for him. And several flying dinosaurs, including Liam circled above, trying to see if they could find Hugo. Perhaps he was injured and had landed somewhere, unable to fly back?

Not satisfied with capturing Dr. Carbon and destroying the Filth Bots, the dinosaurs sprang into action to retrieve the huge treasure trove of evidence housed at the airfield, before it could be removed or destroyed by anyone.

They carefully searched the hundreds of filing cabinets, each brimming with dark secrets. Once forced open, their contents were revealed. What the dinosaurs discovered was really quite shocking. They were full of evidence of over 40 years of corruption and a conspiracy to stop anyone inventing an alternative to oil and gas as a source of energy. It was plain to see - Big Oil and governments around the world had been paying Dr. Carbon to spread lies and false information about climate change and global warming.

The hundreds of dirty and out-of-date computers were also overflowing with classified information, which could now be accessed too and the secret files downloaded. The evidence was extensive and damning. It implicated hundreds of very important people all over the world.

It would be necessary to secure this evidence as it would be needed later, to help prosecute the various high-profile business people and well known world leaders that had been profiteering from their love affair with Big Oil.

The migrant slave workers eventually emerged from their various hiding places around the airfield, with some coaxing from the dinosaurs.

They were absolutely terrified at what was happening. But once the air battle was over and they got over the shock of their deserted, run down home being invaded by hordes of very angry and hostile dinosaurs, they decided to ally themselves with their saviours. They soon realised that they had been saved and that the dinosaurs were actually quite gentle and kind - if you weren't a dirty, smoky Filth Bot.

It took some nerve to surrender themselves to the dinosaurs. But ultimately they reckoned it couldn't possibly be any worse than being enslaved by the dastardly Dr. Carbon.

Their leader, a tall, skinny, Romanian called Florin, approached the dinosaurs and said to them in broken English. "Please helps us! We are starving. What we do now?" He looked desperate. "The Dr. Carbon, he very evil man. He take us all prisoner and force us work for £2 a week. He hardly feed us!"

Once all the migrant workers had given themselves up, they realised they had made the right decision. Astrid arranged for several hundred pizzas to be made with a variety of simple toppings to be flown from the pizza kitchen back in the Welsh cave for the migrants.

Once fed, the migrant workforce helped the dinosaurs clear up the airfield. The dinosaurs told them that they could stay there to live for good and that they would help them to fix up the area and set up a Dino Power turbine to provide free power.

Liam explained to the migrants that they would be able to generate more power than they needed and would be able to sell the excess to the National Grid, just like the dinosaurs did. That way they would have enough income to live a good life and to buy food for them all. Liam even suggested that Oscar might build them a pizza oven if they wanted one.

At this point a small inflatable boat started to approach the coastline near to Dr Carbon's lair, Astrid quickly swam out to intercept it and Liam gave her air cover - in stealth mode, of course.

The hatchet-faced man who drove Dr. Carbon around was at the controls of the boat as it steadily chugged towards the airfield. He was bringing in the next boatload of kidnapped migrants. Liam quickly swooped down and plucked the hatchet-faced from the boat. He carried him to the main hut on the airfield and he was promptly placed under house arrest.

It turned out the man was actually Dr. Carbon's nephew, called Barry. The migrants clearly hated him and quickly tied him to a chair, so that he couldn't escape. Liam had to make sure they didn't harm him and eventually decided to fly him to the cave in Wales, for his own safety more than anything.

The dinosaurs then shared out Dr. Carbon's stash of gold bars, amongst the migrant workers. After all, they had all done the work to earn much of it. Each got two 12.5 kilogram bars, which by Astrid's calculations were worth over £1 million. The bars were very heavy and the weak migrant workers lugged them around with something of a struggle. Many of them stashed both gold bars under their beds.

With Dr. Carbon now securely confined to his rocky cell back at the dinosaurs' cave in Wales, Oscar and his gang confronted him. They demanded answers about his sinister intentions to blow up the entrance to their cave network and to seal them in. They also wanted to know who was behind the conspiracy to protect Big Oil's interests at the risk of destroying the world.

Dr. Carbon remained defiant, his lips sealed, as he brazenly declared, "You'll never get it out of me. I'll never talk. Try what you like. No comment! No comment! No comment!"

However, he had underestimated the dinosaurs' extraordinary intelligence and abilities, particularly their power to read minds. Despite his efforts to hide his thoughts, Olivia, one of the dinosaurs' finest mind readers, skilfully extracted every memory and secret from his brain in less than 15 minutes. He struggled to resist initially, but he was no match for Olivia. She probed into every dark corner of his mind and sucked out every memory.

She was able to reveal every thought and experience from the moment he was born, to his first day at school and his miserable time being bullied as a teenager, right up to conversations about the plot to blow up the dinosaurs' cave...and everything in between.

They also discovered that Dr. Carbon's true name was Horace Potts, and he hailed from the peaceful town of Tunbridge Wells in Kent, UK. His mother had been a school dinner lady at a local school and the other people in his class at school had called him 'Spotty, Potty, Potts.'

Olivia identified extensive evidence of blackmail, bribery, and corruption, with evidence of hefty bribes paid to world leaders, high-ranking officials of state, other senior politicians, and industrialists to keep the world using carbon fuels and plastics.

She also uncovered thousands of covert bank accounts hidden away in Switzerland, containing billions of dollars worth of illicit funds, secretly held by various well-known politicians and other influential world leaders.

They were shocking revelations, and Luna felt furious and disgusted that so many common people were being deceived like this, all for the sake of profit and power.

Luna and Oscar knew that they had to make sure that the truth was exposed fully and the corruption stopped, once and for all. Everything that Dr. Carbon had revealed, when Olivia read his mind, was used to make sense of the files found in his lair. The files contained all the evidence they needed of the blackmail, bribery and corruption that had been going on behind the scenes.

Unfortunately, the process of reading Dr. Carbon's mind and extracting all the information from him had completely scrambled his mind! He would never be able to stand trial in court. He now just spoke complete nonsense and couldn't remember anything of any consequence.

Olivia had tried repeatedly to extract from Dr. Carbon who the shadowy figure was that had been telling him what to do via his headset. But it was clear that Dr. Carbon actually didn't know. It was the only real loose end left to solve but they couldn't work out who it was, try as they might.

News then came in that Hugo's limp body had been found by Astrid, floating in the Atlantic Ocean. One of the Filth Bot's rockets had torn through his body and he had been killed instantly. He had landed in the sea near a small pebble island a few miles from the disused airfield.

Astrid carried Hugo's body back to the cave entrance but couldn't bring herself to bring him inside or to break the terrible news to Oscar. She discreetly spoke to Luna who struggled to control her emotions as she listened to Astrid's description of how she had found him. Luna realised that she would have to find the courage to tell Oscar.

She waved awkwardly to Oscar across the room and gestured to him to follow her into his office. Oscar could sense something was wrong but he wasn't quite sure what.

Once in Oscar's office, Luna shut the door and just blurted it out. "They've found Hugo. I'm afraid he is dead! I'm so sorry Oscar."

Oscar was heartbroken, He openly started to cry. Luna had never seen Oscar like this. He was completely inconsolable. Oscar then blubbed "Oh Luna, he was my first cousin. He is the first of our clan to have died. We will have to create a monument for him here at the cave, to celebrate his life and the sacrifice he made to help save Earth".

After a while Luna led Oscar back to where the rest of the dinosaurs were celebrating their great victory. She held Oscar's hand tightly. Luna realised she was going to have to tell the others what had happened, as Oscar simply couldn't speak.

The other dinosaurs looked devastated at the news. The colour drained from their faces and several cried. Astrid and Alexander hugged Oscar. The room was now completely silent.

After a while Oscar insisted on seeing the body, so he could bring Hugo inside the cave where his body would be safe. They placed him on his bed and placed hundreds of poppies from nearby fields over his still body. A dinosaur guard was placed at his cave door, their heads bowed in solemn respect.

The next day they buried Hugo in a beautiful meadow overlooking the open sea and covered his grave with a tall stack of heavy stones from the surrounding fields and hills. Oscar and Luna both said some kind words, celebrating the wonderful dinosaur that Hugo was.

Oscar held back tears and tried to speak as clearly as he could. "Hugo was my cousin and he was also my friend. All of you that knew him well, know that he was a very quiet, thoughtful and kind dinosaur. I will miss him terribly. He gave his life to help us beat Big Oil and the corrupt people who would risk the Earth in the pursuit of power and profit. Hugo was a true hero and we can learn from him and the sacrifice he has made."

CHAPTER 16

A Time for Justice

Over the next few months, the dinosaurs invested millions of their own money to hire the best legal team from around the world. They wanted to make sure that those individuals who had profited from damaging the planet, and risked the extinction of the human race, faced the consequences of their actions.

They also arranged for another press conference, where their lawyer Sir Jeremy Sharp KC - a King's Counsel - could explain what was happening to the world's press.

Their next destination was The Hague, Netherlands, where The International Court of Justice was located.

After months of relentless effort, the legal team had successfully pulled together and organised the massive piles of evidence and made the details public to the media. The world was left in disbelief at the sheer magnitude of the corruption and the devastating toll it had taken on the environment for so many decades.

The world had also been awakened to the urgency of environmental protection, and people everywhere began to rally for a more sustainable future. Luna and Oscar's relentless pursuit of truth and justice had not only exposed a web of corruption but had also led to the growth of a powerful movement for change, uniting everyone in the face of its greatest challenge yet.

Luna had her fingers crossed. If everything went their way, their plan could mark an end to decades of deceit and greed, and usher in a new era where the Earth and its inhabitants would come first.

Oscar and Luna arrived early for the start of the trial at The International Court of Justice, which is situated in The Hague, Netherlands.

Luna was amazed, she had never seen a building anything quite like it. She felt that the imposing building mirrored the gravity and significance of the proceedings conducted within its hallowed chambers.

The street outside the International Court of Justice in The Hague was busy and lively. People from all walks of life made their way up and down the street, going about their business. Some were dressed formally in suits and ties, while others wore more casual clothes.

As Oscar, the large, pink-feathered dinosaur, strolled down the street, people stopped in their tracks and gazed in astonishment. Some even grabbed their mobile phones to snap pictures of this unusual sight.

Oscar was thoroughly enjoying himself. He smiled broadly at a man sporting clown makeup and a striped T-shirt, who was walking on stilts, while promoting an upcoming circus show. At first, Oscar was taken aback by the towering stilt walker, as he had never seen a human quite so tall. When Luna quickly told him that it was merely a circus trick and that the man had wooden legs he was standing on, Oscar relaxed. The tall man, however, appeared just as astonished as the rest of the people on the street at the appearance of Oscar.

"Hey there, big guy! You're stealing the show with those flashy pink feathers of yours," the stilt-walker exclaimed with a broad smile, his eyes widening.

The crowd around them chuckled at the banter, enjoying the unexpected camaraderie between the towering dinosaur and the stilt-wearing performer.

Luna, who was enjoying the friendly exchange between the two of them, chimed in, "Oscar, I think he means you're turning heads. You are like a fashion statement, but with pink feathers!"

Oscar, embracing the man's playful spirit, slapped a high-five against the stilt walker's hand, causing a ripple of laughter and applause from the onlookers.

The sun was shining brightly overhead, casting a warm glow over everything. It was a beautiful day, and everyone seemed to be in a good mood. It was time for them to make their way into the court. Luna watched with a smile, as Oscar made his way down the street, grateful for the wonderful friend she had by her side.

Once inside the building, they found themselves in a grand entrance hall with high ceilings and ornate decor. The walls were adorned with paintings and sculptures, while the marble floors gleamed with a polished sheen. The air was filled with the scent of fresh flowers and the sound of footsteps echoed loudly through the expansive space.

The courtroom itself was a breathtaking sight. It was a large, oval-shaped room with towering ceilings adorned with grand chandeliers. The walls were elegantly panelled with dark wood, and the floor boasted a polished marble surface.

Upon their arrival at the court, Luna and Oscar were greeted by the sight of 159 corrupt politicians on trial for accepting bribes from Big Oil and 62 high-ranking executives from some of the world's biggest corporations and organisations. And this was probably only the tip of the iceberg.

At the front of the room, the judge sat on a large bench with a gavel resting in front of him. Positioned behind the bench, a large mural depicted a scene from the world of international law. In front of it stood a stately wooden lectern from where the lawyers addressed the court. While waiting for their turns, they sat at smaller desks on either side of the judge as the latter conducted the proceedings.

The public seating area was nothing short of spectacular either, featuring plush chairs adorned in red velvet and offering an unobstructed view of the judges' bench. The walls were decorated with paintings and sculptures, and large windows bathed the room in abundant natural light.

The people within the courtroom were dressed in formal attire. The politicians on trial wore suits and ties, while the judge and lawyers donned black robes. Luna and Oscar occupied seats in the back row of the public benches, keenly observing every unfolding moment.

They couldn't help but feel a bit overwhelmed by the grandiose nature of the building. The magnificent architecture and the lavish interior made them feel small, and to be honest, a tad intimidated.

The courtroom was filled with lawyers, judges, and spectators from around the world. Luna was in awe of the grandeur of the space, with its lofty ceilings and intricate decorations.

The world's media sat outside of the court waiting to report what happened each day. And the whole world waited for a ruling.

The judge stood tall, with a stern look on his face. He sported a thick moustache and a black robe over his suit. Luna and Oscar noticed that he had a nervous tic. He would repeatedly tap his gavel on the desk when anxiety got the better of him.

Luna and Oscar couldn't help but giggle at the judge's nervous tic. It was quite funny to watch him tapping away at the desk over and over again. It kept making everyone in the court including the members of the jury jump! Luna and Oscar made an effort to stifle their giggles, not wanting to disrupt the otherwise serious court proceedings.

Oscar had brought along a couple of pizza slices to snack on while they watched the court proceedings. He offered a slice to Luna, who politely declined when she noticed it had a mealworm and cold custard topping. She felt a bit worried about Oscar eating in the court, but then she remembered that they had let a massive pink dinosaur sit in the courtroom, so munching on strange pizzas was probably the least of their concerns.

Luna watched as Oscar munched on his pizza, trying her best not to laugh at the sight of him eating in court. However, a slight pang of envy crept over her as she wished she had also brought a little something to nibble on during the proceedings.

The trial dragged on for hours, and Luna and Oscar remained seated. It was fascinating in the beginning, but the lengthy proceedings began to take their toll, and Luna found herself feeling a bit drowsy. She fought to stay alert, dead set on not missing a moment of the trial.

Utter pandemonium continued for days and days, as the various revelations and accusations were made. Each day seemed pretty much the same as the next.

"Order! Order please! Order in the court! I will have order in my court," yelled the Judge repeatedly.

The main prosecutor leaned forward purposefully towards the Judge and said, "Your Honor, we have more evidence to present."

One of the defence lawyers quickly protested, "Objection, Your Honor! This is all completely irrelevant!"

One by one, the politicians took their turns on the stand, facing rigorous questioning from the prosecution.

None of them could explain their lavish lifestyles or the numerous homes in multiple locations, including the Caribbean, Monaco, Venice, and the South of France. Several had two or more luxurious super yachts, all of which were seized, along with 14 private jets, 17 helicopters and over 200 luxurious holiday homes.

Luna listened intently as they tried to deny their wrongdoing but the compelling evidence against them left little room for escape.

"I never took any bribes! It's a misunderstanding," protested one President from a South American Country.

"Misunderstanding? How do you explain the 29 offshore accounts, two super yachts and a private jet on a salary of just $48,000 a year?" questioned the prosecuting lawyer.

And so it went on, and on, and on. Hours and hours of claims, counterclaims, points of order and eventually the wrong doers started to crack under pressure and turn on each other.

The President of the United States actually decided to spill the beans on many of the others, in return for an immunity deal with the prosecution, so that he wouldn't have to go to prison.

In total the trial lasted 22 gruelling days, leaving Luna and Oscar utterly exhausted. Luna had carefully followed the arguments presented by both the prosecution and the defence, but it was evident from the very beginning that these high-ranking politicians were guilty of accepting multi-million dollar bribes and kickbacks from Big Oil and Dr. Carbon. In exchange, they had turned a blind eye to the destruction of the environment and the exploitation of vulnerable communities.

Some of the politicians eventually gave up information about their secret Swiss bank accounts, while others remained silent, refusing to reveal where they had hidden their ill-gotten gains. But Luna and Oscar already had all the details of the illegal accounts. Luna and Oscar had already decided that if they refused to cooperate with the Court, and hand over the money, she and Oscar would take action.

If left unseized, they planned to remove the illegal funds and donate them to some of the biggest environmental charities in the world, to help them undo some of the terrible damage that Big Oil had caused to the planet over the years.

The presiding judge delivered a verdict that stunned the courtroom. Over 169 senior politicians and public figures, including two Presidents and four Prime Ministers, were found guilty on counts of accepting bribes and engaging in corrupt behaviour. They were handed lengthy prison sentences, with one of them receiving an 18-year prison term for their role in the scandal.

Their assets were seized and they were ordered to reimburse the ill-gotten gains they had accumulated over the years.

Loud gasps and murmurs swept through the courtroom as the reality of the situation sank in.

Luna felt a mix of emotions as she watched the verdict being delivered. While she was glad that justice had been served, there was also a lingering sadness in her heart. It was clear that these politicians had been motivated by greed and power, and they didn't seem to care about the immense damage they were causing to the planet. As she exited the courtroom alongside Oscar, Luna knew that the fight to protect the Earth was far from over. There was still a lot of work to be done if they were going to make a real difference.

Nevertheless, with the guilty politicians behind bars and the world bearing witness, her determination to carry on the struggle for a brighter future had only grown stronger.

Oscar had already started brainstorming about how to make the best use of the dismantled Filth Bots. He knew that their parts could be repurposed to create equipment that could remove pollution from the environment. It was not going to be easy, but Oscar was sure he could come up with some innovative ways to help heal the planet from the damage caused by Big Oil, Dr Carbon and his Filth Bots.

As Luna began transferring the funds from the still secret Swiss bank accounts to various environmental charities and initiatives, she couldn't help but feel an overwhelming sense of satisfaction for the first time in months. She could only imagine the vast potential for positive change that these funds would have on the environment!

The charities themselves couldn't believe the massive influx of donations from a mysterious anonymous source during this period of time. Some of the smaller charities benefited from 100 times the normal level of donations they would expect in a whole year, in less than a week. The money simply poured into their coffers like a waterfall of cash.

The sum of money was staggering, and she knew it could fund groundbreaking work to fight climate change, support sustainable farming practices, and protect endangered species.

She imagined the beaming faces of children benefiting from better access to clean water and education, all made possible by these newfound funds. They could support the development of innovative technologies for removing carbon, bring struggling coral reefs back to life, and provide vital aid to places destroyed by natural disasters made worse by climate change.

As the last transfer was completed, Luna took a moment to reflect on the incredible journey that had led her here. From uncovering corruption in the darkest corners of the corridors of power, to standing before the International Court of Justice, it had been a tireless pursuit of justice and environmental protection.

Word of the donations quickly spread and Luna found herself receiving inquiries from several media owners eager to hear her story. She agreed to sit for interviews, hoping that by sharing her experiences, she could inspire others to step forward and create positive change in the world. The money donated was referred to as 'Oscar's Behest'.

CHAPTER 17

What to do with Dr. Carbon

L una and Oscar faced a dilemma when it came to deciding what to do with Dr. Carbon. The process of extracting all of Dr. Carbon's memories had a profound impact on him, leaving him with a significant loss of memory. He couldn't recall very much at all from his past, his identity and knowledge had been wiped clean. It was safe to say he posed no further threat to the world.

They had decided not to hand him over to the authorities. He couldn't remember very much anymore and rambled on and on when questioned about his past. Luna couldn't help but feel a twinge of sympathy for him, and anyway, they already knew all about him and the people he had conspired with.

To ensure that he could never cause harm again, Luna proposed an unconventional solution: a trip to Belarus, famed for its supposed title as one of the most boring destinations on the planet, according to recent online surveys. She wasn't all that sure how true this was but it sounded like a good place for Dr Carbon to see out his days.

With an invisible Oscar as his guide, Dr. Carbon found himself deposited just outside a large police station in the busy capital of Minsk. Cars hummed, people buzzed, and street performers begged for money in the street.

Inside the police station, Sergeant Ivanovich, a middle-aged officer, who didn't speak the best English, noticed the dishevelled and disoriented man in a dark suit and tie outside.

Dr. Carbon appeared lost, muttering incomprehensibly.

Concern etched on his face, Sergeant Ivanovich approached the bewildered man, "You, ah, okay? What you do here?" he asked, his English a bit stilted.

Dr. Carbon, still grappling with the remnants of his wiped memories, responded with a vacant stare. Sensing something was off, the Sergeant decided to bring him inside, hoping they could provide some assistance.

Concerned for the deluded English man, the policemen ushered Dr. Carbon into the station, offering him a warm cup of tea and a cheese sandwich. The mismatched conversations unfolded, Sergeant Ivanovich attempting to communicate, "Tea, good for...eh, calming," in his limited English.

Dr. Carbon, still dazed and disoriented, accepted the refreshments, staring blankly at the walls of the police station. The officers and the translator exchanged glances, realising this man needed more than a hot drink and a sandwich.

They were puzzled by the man's peculiar behaviour and incomprehensible speech since they didn't understand English very well. However, they eventually found a translator and soon realised that the man was suffering from severe delusions.

The translator relayed a strange and disjointed tale of flying dinosaurs and a supposed friendship with the U.S. President. The police officers exchanged bemused glances, realising they had an unusual case on their hands.

Sergeant Ivanovich, torn between confusion and concern, muttered to himself in Russian, "Crazy day in Minsk," as the man who once threatened the survival of the world now stood confused and harmless.

Concern etched on his face, Sergeant Ivanovich murmured to his colleague, "Something not right. Maybe, uh, need help. Special help."

And so, a call was made to the local mental health institute. The officers knew they were out of their depth and needed professionals to handle this peculiar case.

Oscar, watching from the shadows, felt a mix of emotions. Despite Dr. Carbon's sinister past, Oscar couldn't ignore the state of the man's current mental health. He had seen the inner workings of the man's tormented mind during the interrogation back at the cave.

As the police escorted Dr. Carbon away, Oscar wished for the man to find the help he desperately needed to mend his fractured life and to find peace.

The sun dipped below the horizon, casting long shadows across the city streets. Oscar, contemplating the events he had witnessed, knew it was time to return to his cave home back in the Welsh hills, for a well-deserved rest. He soared through the skies, mindful to avoid a passing plane filled with oblivious holidaymakers.

Down on the streets of Minsk, a truck arrived, its team gently placing Dr. Carbon in the back of the vehicle. With a low hum, the truck navigated the city streets, eventually heading toward their destination.

Oscar, maintaining a watchful eye on the truck, soared above as it sped along.

A young boy in the passing passenger plane, catching a glimpse of the massive pink dinosaur, excitedly tried to share the sighting with his mother. However, this met with a stern response from his mother.

"Don't be ridiculous," she scolded. "Pink flying dinosaurs! That'll be the day."

Little did she know, the day had already dawned in a world where dinosaurs flew once more and conspiracies crumbled.

CHAPTER 18

Recognition from a Grateful World

Soaring higher into the night sky, Oscar couldn't help but marvel at the glittering lights below, each one a little beacon of life in the vast expanse of the planet. The cool breeze whistled past him, carrying the scents of adventure and the promise of home. The Welsh mountains awaited and Oscar couldn't be more thrilled.

Gliding through the night, Oscar felt the anticipation building with each passing moment. And as the familiar silhouette of his cave emerged in the moonlight, a comforting sight against the rugged peaks and whispering trees.

Touching down just outside the cave, he couldn't resist taking a moment to soak up the natural world around him. The crisp air, the scent of pine, and the distant murmur of babbling streams.

As he entered the cave, the dim glow of light and the rhythmic beats of hip hop music guided him forward. Luna, with a smile that could light up the cave itself, welcomed him with a tight hug.

"Oscar, you're back! Did you bring any cool souvenirs?" asked Luna.

Winking as he replied, Oscar said "You know it! Wait till you see what I've got," as he revealed a selection of beautiful hand painted scarves for Luna and the others.

Inside the cave, the atmosphere was simply joyous. Astrid, Alexander, and the other dinosaurs joined the reunion, their eyes twinkling with delight.

"Come on Oscar, spill the beans! Any thrilling tales from your latest adventure?" asked Astrid.

"Oh, you won't believe the things I've seen," answered Oscar, grinning broadly, thinking of the mother telling her son off in the plane for simply telling her what he had seen with his own two eyes.

And so, the night unfolded into a delightful gathering. They formed a circle, sharing stories that echoed through the cave. Laughter bubbled up like a spring, and memories of their global escapades filled the air. To celebrate, they decided to have a huge party. They agreed to invite dinosaurs from every one of their secret cave headquarters. They also decided to create all the decorations out of the many tonnes of rubbish they had collected over the past year or two.

In the days that followed, the cave became a hive of creativity. Luna, Oscar, and their friends transformed discarded treasures into vibrant decorations.

Broken bottles became lanterns, old banners turned into streamers, and metal scraps morphed into quirky sculptures.

"Our home is going to be the coolest cave in the world!" announced Luna.

The culmination of their efforts was the grand party. Invitations were extended to every furry, feathery, and scaly dino friend.

The cave was transformed into a wonderland, with additional cozy seating areas for the dinosaurs and an extended dance floor made of polished stones and sparkling crystals.

Excitement radiated through the cave as the day of the party arrived. The aroma of freshly baked pizzas filled the air, and the chatter of friends mingled with the fizz of colas and the formal bowing that tended to follow any drinking of cola.

"To home, to friends, and to more adventures!" proclaimed Oscar, raising a large slice of the finest pizza.

And so, in the heart of the Welsh mountains, their cave echoed with the joyous laughter of dinosaurs and the warmth of true companionship.

As the party entered full swing, Luna couldn't help but wonder about Noah. He hadn't replied to the party invitation she had sent him, and they didn't expect him to make it.

Little did they know that he had a surprise in store for them. Suddenly, the huge rock blocking the cave's entrance rolled aside, and to everyone's amazement, there stood Noah, grinning ear to ear. Luna leaped up in joy, running to wrap him in a tight hug.

With Noah's unexpected entrance, the party continued with even more laughter, music, and dancing.

As the party progressed, Luna stumbled upon an unexpected and very official looking letter on Oscar's desk, and as she tore it open, her eyes widened.

It was an invitation to the United Nations, complete with news of a prestigious award for their extraordinary efforts in battling corruption and championing environmental causes. Luna couldn't contain her excitement and sprinted to share the news with the entire gang, including Oscar, who was thrilled at the thought of a trip to New York City.

"Hey guys, we're going to the United Nations! We've won an award!" Luna blurted out breathlessly.

"Well, ain't that fancy? Do we get to wear tuxedos?" proposed Oscar, grinning.

"Do they have a category for 'Best Dinosaur Performance'?" asked Astrid.

"No, but they should! And, Oscar, you can wear a tux if you want," answered Luna helpfully.

Now there really was an excuse to party.

And so, with the echoes of one of Oscar's favourite songs ringing in their ears from the sound system, Oscar suddenly broke into a celebratory rap.

Oscar's Rap

Yo, it's Oscar the Dino, listen up, gather 'round, Back to Earth I came, on a mission profound. Landed in a world, full of trouble and strife, humans needed help, so I brought the dino hype.

Met Luna and Noah, they were cool as can be, Joined forces together, now we a fierce family. Dr. Carbon and his filthy bots, thought they had it all, but we stood tall, ready for the brawl.

Oscar's in the house, stomping on the ground, Dino Power's rising, hear the roaring sound. Luna, Noah, and me, a team so tight, saving the Earth, making everything right.

Dr. Carbon's conspiracy, oh what a mess, Tried to silence us all, create distress. Filth Bots everywhere, spreading hate and fear, but we didn't back down, we just shifted up a gear.

Dinos on a mission, stomping with pride, Luna by our side, nowhere to hide. Noah's cracking jokes, making us smile, together we go that extra mile.

Oscar's in the house, stomping on the ground, Dino Power's rising, hear the roaring sound. Luna, Noah, and me, a team so tight, saving the Earth, making everything right.

Touring the world, day and night, Spreading the word, doing things right. No more Big Oil, no more crazy power schemes, just eco-friendly dreams, in our Dino Power regime.

Fame and fortune, knocking on our door, Dino Power booming, we're wanting more. Saving the planet, making it green, Oscar's the king, ruling supreme.

Dr. Carbon defeated, Filth Bots destroyed, The world rejoiced, in the peace we deployed. Humans and dinosaurs, side by side, in this eco-revolution, there's nothing to hide.

Oscar's in the house, stomping on the ground, Dino Power's rising, hear the roaring sound. Luna, Noah, and me, a team so tight, Saving the Earth, making everything right.

So here's the tale of Oscar's Rap, Dinos and humans, closing the gap. We're the guardians of Earth, in a rhythm so sweet, Dino Power anthem, can't be beat!

THE END

Printed in Great Britain
by Amazon

0566438f-5471-4c42-943c-6944d0013223R01